Rangeland Detective

GEORGE J. PRESCOTT

A Black Horse Western

ROBERT HALE · LONDON

© George J. Prescott 2003
First published in Great Britain 2003

ISBN 0 7090 7305 4

Robert Hale Limited
Clerkenwell House
Clerkenwell Green
London EC1R 0HT

The right of George J. Prescott to be identified as
author of this work has been asserted by him
in accordance with the Copyright, Design and
Patents Act 1988.

*To the memory of my Grandfather
and his old enemy "Big Chief One Eye"*

Typeset by
Derek Doyle & Associates, Liverpool.
Printed and bound in Great Britain by
Antony Rowe Limited, Wiltshire

CHAPTER ONE

Desert nights are cold and the man hunkered by the glow of the minute fire, gratefully shrugged deeper into his sheepskin as he watched his companion carefully turning the irons he had earlier placed in the heart of the red glow.

He glanced across the camp ground, which was only fitfully illuminated by the firelight, to the man they had caught earlier, spread-eagled on a flattish piece of ground, wrists and ankles tied to stakes with well-wetted rawhide. He'd lain in the sun since noon, and as the man in the sheepskin approached him, the cracked lips moved.

'Water,' the tortured man croaked and the smaller cowboy by the fire laughed shortly,

'Ain't gonna be water he'll be abegging for soon,' he said, carefully lifting an iron from the fire and inspecting its glowing end. His taller companion offered no reply as he squatted easily by the prisoner's side.

Abruptly, he slapped the man's face and the prisoner jerked, eyes snapping open.

'Glad you're still with us,' the man in the sheepskin

sneered. 'Now I'm gonna ask you agin about the money, and this time you better remember or . . .' he gestured towards the fire. His victim screamed as he saw the smaller man stand and swing the glowing end of a running iron towards him.

'There's some,' the small man said reasonably, 'who say a stamping-iron is best. Me, I figure it leaves too much of a mark. Now this,' he continued, matter-of-factly jabbing the glowing end into the bound man's leg and drawing a scream of agony, 'this don't leave any mark a man'd be able to swear to.' Appetite gleamed in his eyes for a moment as he said, 'I hope you ain't in no hurry to talk, friend, 'cause you and me, we got all night.'

Impatiently, the big man in the sheepskin waved his companion away.

'Now look,' he began, almost gently. 'You can see how it is. We want to know where the money is. Tell us and I'll finish it quick and clean. Otherwise. . . .' the gesture was enough and the bound man screamed hysterically.

'But I've told you, as God is my judge, all the letter said was the cave below the Eagle's Claw.'

'Ain't no cave called that around here,' the smaller man by the fire insisted.

'N-No,' the other agreed, his Eastern accent out of place in the New Mexican desert, 'b-but . . . God, give me a drink of water, I can't talk no more.'

The drink, a mere moistening of the lips, appeared to revive the dying man and he croaked:

'I went to the cave, but there was nothing there! No gold, nothing.'

'Mebbe it weren't the cave?' the big man suggested, his voice ominously quiet,

'No.' The other shook his head. 'There was plenty of sign that someone had used it for a hideout. Not for some time, but then they hung Levi Levinson at El Paso five years ago, him and three of his boys, so you'd expect that.'

'But no gold?' the big man demanded and the prisoner shook his head. Slowly, the Easterner's tormentor rose to his feet and stretched, staring at the ground speculatively.

Thoughtfully, he reached up and scratched under the band of his Stetson before methodically spitting in the prisoner's face.

'Collins, you're a liar,' the big man stated easily. 'I think you took that coin and hid it. Sato,' he finished, turning to his companion, 'you try. See if you kin get the truth outta him.'

Dawn was pearling the sky when Sato unceremoniously shook his companion awake. The big man twisted in his blankets.

'Well?' he demanded blearily. Sato shrugged, nervously dropping a hand to his holstered Colt.

'Cashed,' he said, tightly. ' I figure mebbe he didn't know nothin' after all.' His companion sat up, rubbing sleep from his eyes and reached across to throw off his coverings.

'Guess you're right, Sato,' he offered blearily, right hand disappearing casually beneath a blanket. There was the sudden crack of a shot and Sato pawed convulsively at his chest before subsiding to the ground without a sound. His killer crouched over him, gun ready, but with a convulsive clutch at the other's fancy vest, Sato jerked and was still.

Callously, the killer glanced at the sky, then with a shrug of resignation turned to the pack-horse for a shovel. Collins and Sato would have to be planted and, in anticipation of hot work to come, he shrugged off his vest, the morning sunlight glinting on the star pinned there as he did so.

Rich Blagg was another who didn't like loose ends, his own or anybody else's. As he sat in the sumptuous office he maintained above the Busted Dollar, the only saloon to grace the little trail-town of Waco's Find, he was concerned about one loose end in particular, which might start to unravel in a very inconvenient direction.

Somewhat appalled by the path his thoughts had been taking, he slammed a meaty palm on to the bell on his desk. When the duty bartender put his head around the door, Blagg snarled:

'Rolo back yet?'

The barman nodded. 'Just got in, boss,' he said, adding incautiously, 'You want to see him now?'

'No, goddamit,' Blagg flared. 'I wanted to see the son of a bitch yesterday.' He cursed again at his employee's carefully blank look and stormed: 'Send that bastard up here now, Marty, then get back to work!'

Blagg was studying a document at his desk when Rolo slouched in and unceremoniously slumped into a chair. After a moment, Blagg tossed the document aside and snapped:

'Well, where's Collins?'

Rolo shrugged, concentrating on the cigarette he was rolling.

'Dunno,' he mumbled, carefully licking the brown paper and pushing the finished product through his beard and into his mouth. He scratched a match, ignoring the fuming Blagg and touched the end of his smoke. He shrugged again and said:

'He give me the slip.'

'He's a city boy and he give you the slip?' Blagg snorted disbelievingly. 'How?'

'Dunno,' Rolo mumbled again, eyes shifting towards his boots. Blagg regarded him thoughtfully for a moment, mind working furiously. What Rolo had said wasn't as unlikely as it might have sounded to a stranger. Rolo had his uses, particularly in a bar-room, but when it came to outside work, he was barely able to get himself around the town without getting lost.

'OK,' Blagg said eventually, 'so you lost him. What are you going to do about it?'

'Find him. Mebbe he went back to El Paso,' Rolo offered stupidly.

'Mebbe,' Blagg admitted grudgingly,' or mebbe not. Know anyone who might be able to find him . . . wherever he is?' he asked.

'What about Marvin?' Rolo offered. Blagg laughed, a short harsh bark.

'No,' he said. 'Our beloved marshal couldn't find his ass with both hands.'

Rolo looked sheepish, then said slowly: 'Heard about a fella while I was up in 'Paso last year. Name of Wheeler, Cord Wheeler. He's what they call a private detective and he's got quite a rep for finding missing

9

RANGELAND DETECTIVE

folk. Like a Pinkeye,' he explained as the look of puzzlement crossed Blagg's face.' He's a cripple, but he's supposed to be good.'

'Bounty hunter?' the saloonkeeper sneered.

Rolo shook his head. 'No,' he answered, 'he don't just find guys who are wanted. Husbands, wives, kids, you know.' Rolo shrugged helplessly, cudgelling his less than agile brain until the phrase suddenly popped in. 'Missing persons was what the flyer I saw said, and,' Rolo added significantly,' he ain't the law.'

'Sounds all right,' Blagg admitted, grinning evilly. 'And whether Collins made it back to El Paso or not, this guy shouldn't have any trouble finding him. Let's just hope he ain't too honest, if he comes lookin' down here.'

'Still, we can't just spring this on him,' the fat man continued. 'Have to dress it up some.' He thought for a moment, then thumped a hand on the bell.

When Marty appeared, Blagg said simply:

'Mona. Now.' Turning to Rolo, Blagg sneered: 'This should be just up her alley. Or mebbe down her gutter,' he finished with a leer.

The girl Marty showed in might have been pretty in the half-light of a bar-room, but time and other, less savoury things had coarsened her skin and hair and emphasized the hard lines around an already weak mouth. Blagg explained his proposition briefly and when he'd finished, Mona asked simply:

'What's this Collins look like?'

'Tallish, skinny, black hair with one of those little brush moustaches. Oh, and his right hand's only got three fingers,' Blagg explained. 'You know him?'

10

Mona shook her head nervously. 'No,' she admitted uneasily. 'When should I leave for El Paso?'

'Mornin' stage'll do,' said Blagg expansively. Abruptly, his manner hardened. Slowly, he took a small green medicine-bottle out of the desk and shook it so that the angled facets caught the light.

'Don't forget, darlin', nobody double-crosses me,' Blagg snarled. 'Not Collins and especially not something like you. At least, they don't never do it twice.' He shook the green bottle again, spitefully. 'So you be real careful, won't you, darlin'? Otherwise, mebbe, no more candy.'

When the girl had gone, Rolo said casually:

'You sure made her sit up, Rich. What was in that bottle?'

Blagg settled back. 'I don't overlook no bets, Rolo. It's just a little something Mona don't like to do without.'

Carefully, Rolo said: 'Must be pretty good, boss?'

Blagg laughed, a short vicious bark. 'Sure,' he said, 'only for candy, you could say laudanum. She's an addict, gotta have it. Do anything for it, too,' Blagg finished nastily, raising an eyebrow at the grinning Rolo.

'So she should be safe enough, then,' Rolo asked. 'Ain't likely to open her mouth to Wheeler?'

Blagg shrugged self satisfied shoulders. 'What if she does?' he sneered. 'Even you should be able to handle a cripple!'

Funnily enough, cripple wasn't usually a word people applied to Cord Wheeler. At least, not out loud.

11

He had business in the Busted Flush saloon and dance-hall that evening and Sam Meadows, the head bartender, looked up from his newspaper to find Wheeler standing across the bar from him. Meadows saw a man of average height, dressed in a neat broad-cloth suit, leaning on a brass-knobbed ebony cane. A man you wouldn't look at twice, maybe a well-to-do clerk or small businessman. Except a second look would take in the hardness of the body under the broadcloth and the faint scar that decorated the left cheek. And the eyes. Cold and green like arctic seas and at least a million years old. No clerk ever had eyes like that. But the voice, when Wheeler spoke, was at odds with the scarred face. It was soft and gentle, with still a hint of the courtliness of New Orleans.

'I'd be obliged if I could see Miz Lace, Mr Meadows,' Wheeler asked softly.

Meadows nodded. 'I gotta ask Lancey,' he offered and moved along the bar to where a big man in an expensive suit was lowering the level in a bottle of cheap brandy. He looked up as Meadows addressed him, glanced briefly at Wheeler, then shook his head and threw the contents of another glass down his throat.

Reluctantly, Meadows turned back but he needn't have bothered. Wheeler shifted the weight of his body awkwardly to the stick in his left hand and limped slowly the length of the bar, halting a bare arm's length from the brandy-drinker. His voice was mild as he asked:

'Be obliged if you'd tell Miz Lace I'm here. Name's Wheeler, Cord Wheeler. You might say I can save her some trouble.'

The big man paused with the glass nearly to his lips.

'Her charity day is Thursday,' he sneered, lifting the glass to his reflection. 'All the blind men and cripples and other beggars come round then.' The words were barely out of his mouth before there was a whistling in the air in front of his face and something smashed into his hand, showering him with glass and cheap brandy. He flung round, hand driving under his coat, only to stop as he found himself looking down the rock-steady bore of Cord Wheeler's Smith & Wesson. Wheeler was still leaning easily on his cane and his voice was still mild as he said,

'Mebbe we don't need to bother Miss Lace, I want to see your girls, all of 'em. No, don't bother yourself, Lancey,' Wheeler stated. 'Mr Meadows can fetch 'em.' There might have been an edge to his voice now as Wheeler added: 'Now'd be a good time, Mr Meadows. And I'd advise you to keep your hands where I can see 'em, Lancey.' Wheeler paused but whatever he was going to say was lost in the stentorian bellow which erupted from the balcony overlooking the bar-room.

'And what in the name of Christ and all his little angels makes you think you're gonna get away with lookin' over my girls, Cord Wheeler?'

CHAPTER TWO

Wheeler apparently paid no attention to the shout, nor to the statuesque figure descending the stairs.

'Since Miz Lace is here now, Lancey,' he began courteously, 'you just oblige me by puttin' your hands on your head and then kneeling down about there.'

'I'll be goddamned . . .' Lancey began, but he was interrupted by the crack of Cord Wheeler's pistol and the abrupt removal of his left heel, which knocked him to one knee. Glowering and cursing shakily, he shifted until both knees were under him before carefully putting his hands behind his head. He hadn't even seen Wheeler aim the pistol and any man who could shoot that well wasn't someone to take chances with.

'Excellent,' Wheeler offered. 'Mr Meadows, you just sashay behind him and take his little gun. And, Mr Meadows,' Wheeler finished softly, 'be real careful. Good bartenders are some hard to find and I'd hate to see Miz Lace in any more trouble than she is already. And don't forget to git them young ladies out here. All of them.'

By the time Meadows had assembled the women,

14

Lace Tucker had reached the bottom of the stairs and was standing watching Lancey with a curling lip.

'What are you looking for, Wheeler?' she demanded.

'Why, a girl, Miz Lace.' Wheeler answered easily as he crossed the board floor so as to keep Lancey and Sam Meadows under his gun while he scanned the faces of the saloon workers. They were the usual hard-faced, virtueless harpies normally employed in south-western saloons, even in a big city like El Paso. The one exception looked back at Wheeler without expression, no trace of any emotion in her pretty sixteen-year-old face.

Without taking his eyes from Lancey or Lace Tucker, Wheeler said gently:

'What's your name, miss?' For a moment the girl ignored him, then a confused look chased itself across her face.

'I . . . why my name is Josie.' She looked at Wheeler in disbelief. 'I . . . I . . .' Without heat, Wheeler interrupted, softly, his gaze sweeping the two men under his gun.

'Lancey, you keep still, son. And Mr Meadows, put your hands back on the bar and move away from that sawed-off.' With a smile, he continued: 'Ma'am, you just walk through them doors and you'll find your papa waiting.' Gently, he pushed the girl towards the swinging doors of the saloon and the grey-haired figure framed there against the light, before turning back to Lace Tucker, who had stood by, silent and fuming throughout this exchange.

'If the rest of my boys had been here, you wouldn't damn well have got away with this,' she snarled between clenched teeth.

Wheeler nodded. 'Yes, ma'am,' he offered courteously, 'that was why I waited 'til I saw 'em ride out this afternoon. After I sent you that note from your foreman about the . . . eh . . . round-up, shall we say? Good evenin', ma'am. Oh, and afore I forget,' the voice was still mild but there was an icy chill in it that grated across Lace Tucker's spine, hardened though she was.

'If I hear about this happening again,' he gestured after the stumbling girl and her relieved parent, 'or the Chinaman visitin' this establishment, I'll come back. And, while I could never bring myself to threaten a lady, let me just say that neither you nor Woo Lee'll have the slightest interest in the outcome of any argument I have with your hired boys. Nor with your bed-boy here. Absolutely no interest at all. You have my personal guarantee upon that. Now, ma'am, if you would come this way.'

For a moment, Lace stood undecided, then she snarled: 'Lancey, are you gonna let him get away with this?'

'Sure he is,' Wheeler stated icily, ' 'less he wants another navel.'

Face twisting, Lancey pulled his hands away from his head, only to stop abruptly when a bullet from Wheeler's pistol drilled a hole in the floor a whisker away from his left knee.

'That's the last one I'm wasting on you,' the detective said levelly. 'I hope you ain't stupid enough to think I don't mean it. . . .'

Suddenly, without warning, Wheeler swivelled, firing almost before he had completed his turn. The bar in front of Sam Meadows exploded into fragments and the bartender screamed, dropping the shotgun he had been about to use and staring in disbelief at the foot-long splinter sticking out of his lacerated right hand. Without any apparent interruption in the flow of his movements, Wheeler swivelled at the hip and chopped the lead-weighted tip of his cane into the side of Lancey's head as the bouncer began to rise clumsily to his feet. Lancey dropped without a sound, and Wheeler said mildly:

'I think that's about all, Miz Lace,' he motioned carefully, 'if you'd just come this way.'

Swiftly, Wheeler stepped backwards through the swinging doors, his movements covered by Lace Tucker's body. Moments later, a thin melody drifted in from the street. Someone was whistling *Shenandoah*.

Late the following afternoon Mollie Simpson, Ira Simpson's pretty wife, showed the woman in to Wheeler's combined sitting-room and office, situated above the Simpsons' prosperous store.

'Lady to see yez, Mr Wheeler.' Mollie sniffed, motioning the woman through the door and swiftly closing it after her, without waiting for acknowledgement.

Wheeler rose heavily from his desk, passing a hand through his hair to stem the gathering weight of tiredness. He'd put Josie and her father on a homeward-bound freight at four in the morning and since then, bed had proved elusive. Also his right leg was aching. It always did when he had to spend a lot of time faking the limp.

The limp had appeared, along with the cane, when Wheeler had got out of prison and set up as a detective.

17

People stayed quiet around big bad lawmen, but a mild cripple leaning on a cane evoked nothing but sympathy and a desire to talk. Also, outlaws and badmen tended to treat him with contempt.

At least, until it was too late to make any difference.

He sometimes thought, in his less sober moments, that perhaps he should be grateful to old Chico.

After all, if he hadn't conned Wheeler into that alley and fired the shotgun at him, he'd still be working as a thirty-and-found deputy. Not, of course, that that had kept Wheeler from blowing his head off, anyway, while he was still struggling to cock the hammer of the second barrel.

And it might just have been bad luck, someone whomping him on the head and him coming round to find Chico Martinez's brains all over the alley and his Smith & Wesson the only piece in sight. Of course, that hadn't been the way the jury saw it. Or Ruth.

Awkwardly, with much of his weight on the cane, he bowed and motioned the woman to a seat across the desk, before resuming his chair.

'Mr Wheeler,' she began, in a Southern drawl that was almost convincing, 'I am here because I have heard that you undertake tasks of a delicate nature without the necessity of involving the authorities.'

Wheeler bowed. 'Anything legal, ma'am.' he agreed.

'Just so.' The expensively gloved hands were ringing the fine lace of the handkerchief into ruins as the woman continued: 'My name is Collins, Mr Wheeler, Amanda Collins. My husband, Thaddeus, is a surveyor for the government. Some time ago he was sent to a little town in New Mexico, to survey the route of a new spur line.'

'What town, Miz Collins?' Wheeler asked.

'It was called Waco's Find,' she said. Apparently overcome, the woman dabbed at her eyes and sobbed. 'Oh, Mr Wheeler, I haven't had a letter from him in weeks and ... and ... I'm so worried. His last letter came from El Paso and I thought you might be able to find him ... if he was here ... or ... that other place....' She trailed off and Wheeler nodded sympathetically, eyes narrowing.

'Was there anything in his other letters? Any hint of ... anything?' he asked. Amanda Collins looked up.

'You mean another woman?' The look of shock was well done, and Wheeler's face was carefully immobile as he went on.

'Well, it's one possibility,' he admitted, before asking innocently: 'Could I see the other letters, Miz Collins?'

'Uh ... oh ... uh ... I didn't bring them,' she offered hesitantly, adding swiftly to forestall the obvious question, 'In fact, I really couldn't be sure where they are.'

Wheeler nodded. 'Well, never mind, ma'am. Have you looked around town for him?' he asked and when the woman shook her head, he said gently, 'Perhaps, if I could take down a few details, a description and sich. And I usually ask for an advance payment. For expenses, you understand.'

Amanda Collins nodded. 'How much?' she asked.

'One hundred dollars,' Wheeler returned blandly.

For half an hour after the woman calling herself Amanda Collins had left, Wheeler sat smoking in the battered chair behind the even more disreputable desk, rereading the description of the three-fingered man she had left and grimacing at the sickening memories the words kindled.

Could it be. . . ?

Occasionally, he consulted one of his innumerable scrap-books, until a need for coffee drove him down stairs.

Mollie Simpson barely looked up as Wheeler swung easily into her spotless kitchen. There was no sign of the cane and the limp was gone as he collected a cup and helped himself from the eternally simmering pot on the stove.

It wasn't until he was sitting across the scrubbed boards from her that he spoke and then it was to voice an apparent irrelevance.

'The lady you showed up this morning, Mollie darlin'. What would you say that dress she was wearing would've cost her?'

'Plenty,' Mollie Simpson returned shortly. 'Was it a job?'

Briefly, Wheeler explained and when he had finished, Mollie snorted and shrugged strong and attractively shaped shoulders.

'Her story's as full o' holes as a Chinaman's bucket. That dress would've cost a government man a year's pay, mebbe more. And she didn't keep her husband's letters! Pah, I got every word Ira ever wrote me, and it ain't much, believe me. Any woman'd sooner part with her hair than her husband letters!'

' 'Less'n she don't care about him,' Wheeler offered quietly.

Mollie stared hard at him. 'Why'd she be looking for him then?' she demanded, before realization dawned.

'We're talking about Mrs Collins, Cord,' she snapped to hide her feelings. 'And Ruth did care. It was that sweet-talkin' bastard conned her into runnin' away. Who's to blame! If I could just. . . !'

'Forget it, Mollie,' Wheeler interrupted softly, adroitly changing the subject. 'You think this Miz Collins ain't on the level?'

Mollie Simpson shook her curly head. 'Was Sitting Bull an Indian?' she demanded.

'Way I figured it my own self,' Wheeler admitted as he rose from the table. 'Only thing is, so far that story has cost her exactly one hundred simoleons. And another thousand if I find her husband.' He drew the money from an inner pocket and surveyed it for a moment. Then he shrugged, counted out twenty dollars and dropped the rest on the table.

'Better pay off some of Ira's gamblin' buddies, Mollie darlin',' he said and was gone before she could think of a suitable reply. She did think of something else, though, which had her knocking on his door some minutes later.

'Ain't no more cash, Mollie darlin'.' Wheeler said blandly, raising his hands above his head. 'I'm clean, honest.'

She waved the joke aside, worry plain in her eyes.

'What are you gonna do about this job, Cord?' she demanded, then stopped. His old carpet-bag was open on the desk and a spare shirt and the long barrelled Colt with the shoulder stock that he used instead of a rifle lay next to it. His intention was plain and there was a little break in her voice as she said:

'You're going down there, then?'

21

Wheeler nodded. 'Sure,' he admitted. 'That lady and her story have got me real interested. Not to mention her money.'

Next morning both cane and limp were very much in evidence again as he stood waiting for the train which would take him on the first stage of his journey to the little nothing in the desert known as Waco's Find.

As usual, Wheeler was playing a hunch. Whatever the woman's motives, he was sure that her reasons, or rather the reasons of the person paying her, were not of the purest. They certainly wanted Collins found but the reason they wanted him lay in Waco's Find, not El Paso. And anyone willing to pay over a thousand dollars for the privilege must figure Collins, if that was his name, was worth a whole hell of a lot more. Wheeler had his own ideas about that as well as the real identity of the missing surveyor, the man who called himself Thaddeus Collins.

He was trying unsuccessfully to explain this to Ira and Mollie as he led Hassan, his chunky half-Arab stallion, into the waiting freight car.

'Just be careful,' Mollie snapped, when he'd finished. Brushing angrily at her eyes, she stalked off down the platform.

'I ain't saying that a thousand bucks is something you want to pass up,' said Ira Simpson, gazing after his wife, 'but this one sure smells bad, Cord.'

Wheeler shrugged. 'They probably ain't expectin' me, figuring I'll look around here first,' he explained. 'And . . .'

'And?' Ira prompted.

'Like I said, I've just got a feelin' about this one. It

may be nothin' but then again ... hell, I figure it's worth the train ride,' Wheeler admitted.

Ira nodded, carefully pulling tight the last strap holding Hassan in his stall. He was too familiar with his friend's hunches to ask any more.

'Good luck,' he said quietly, holding out a calloused hand. Wheeler returned the steely grip and said soberly:

'Thanks. I'm hoping I won't need it.'

CHAPTER THREE

On the train south Wheeler began to have doubts. After all, if the man calling himself Collins was there for the reason Wheeler thought, he'd be very careful not to let that knowledge slip out. And if Collins's search hadn't become common knowledge, why would anyone be hunting a penniless ex con? And there was always the distinct possibility that Collins wasn't who Wheeler thought at all.

But then there was that other thing he'd found in his files, the thing that had shot the little one-horse town of Waco's Find to fame all those years ago. None of it seemed to make much sense, so Wheeler tipped his hat across his face and slept until the conductor's voice summoned him to change trains.

Hassan was used to freight cars and gave no trouble, so the next stage of the journey, in the little three-car cattle train, was uneventful and morning found the pair jogging easily along the plain trail that led from the railroad crossing to the little desert stage-stop-cum-trailtown that was Waco's Find.

They were both hot and dusty when Wheeler pulled

up outside the town's only hotel late in the afternoon. It was the usual back country atrocity, clapboard held together with a few nails and a lot of hope. The man from El Paso surveyed the warped boards and filthy windows with a jaundiced eye, before shrugging and flipping Hassan's reins over the hitch rail. He had walked heavily up two of the three steps leading to the boardwalk, when he thought better of it, returned, and tied the reins in a careful slip-knot. Hassan was absolutely reliable and could do tricks that would have turned a circus horse green with envy but. . . .

'No need to advertise,' Wheeler informed the horse as he rubbed a silky muzzle which was thrusting expectantly at his pockets.

No clerk was visible in the dirty interior, nor any bell, but after Wheeler's third roar, he heard a shuffling from the back room and a frowzy little man pushed a well-greased head around the doorframe and snapped:

'Well, what d'you want?'

'Like a room and a place for my pony, if that ain't too much trouble,' Wheeler answered diffidently. Gone was the New Orleans accent and the neat suit of broadcloth. From the voice to his clothes, covered by the full-skirted duster coat and the worn gun belt holding the plain, long-barrelled Colt, Wheeler looked and sounded like any other New Mexican cowboy out of work and down on his luck.

Or so the clerk must have thought and showed by his next question.

'You got money?'

'S-s-sure,' Wheeler mumbled. 'Pay you a week in advance for me and my horse.'

The little man behind the bar sniffed suspiciously as he looked at the tendered coins.

'Livery's down the street,' he said more reasonably. 'Room'll cost you a dollar a week, with meals.'

'What's the food like?' Wheeler began casually, leaning his weight on the bar and shifting his right foot on to the brass rail.

'Wouldn't give it to a dog myself,' the little man said frankly, 'I allus feed at Martha's down the street. You pays a dollar whether you feed here or not, though,' he finished warningly.

'Sure, sure,' Wheeler answered, massaging an aching thigh muscle. 'I was lookin' for a fella,' he continued, and, as he saw the cogs begin to click in the mind of the other, said smoothly, 'He's been away from home a while and his wife asked me to get a message to him. Name o' Collins.' Something in his voice must have grated because the clerk looked up and asked:

'Friend of yours?'

Wheeler shook his head and the clerk continued warily:

'Sure, he was here. Left without payin' his bill so we're holdin' his stuff. You gonna take care of it?'

Wheeler shook his head. 'Nope,' he said,' but I'll telegraph his wife and see if she wants his gear.'

The clerk shrugged. 'Just so's the bill gets paid,' he grumbled.

Characteristically, like the cowboy he had been, Wheeler shared his conclusions with Hassan, while he rubbed the tough little pony down.

'So he was here, ol' hoss,' he mused, 'and he left

26

sudden. Question is, o' course, did he jump or was he pushed?' Hassan snorted and bared his teeth. Wheeler patted the sleek neck and grinned.

'You ain't no help at all,' he said with mock severity. Abruptly, he stopped, aware of a figure that had moved into the afternoon shadow thrown by the big door. It paused for a moment and then a cracked old voice said wearily:

'Find everything you want?'

Wheeler looked over his shoulder, to find the owner of the voice slouching noisily into the barn. He was an old man, dressed in clean, horse-smelling range clothes and he approached Hassan cautiously, rubbing a gentle, calloused hand along the pony's hard flank before chuckling inanely.

'Good li'l pony,' he wheezed and Wheeler found himself looking into a pair of steel-bright eyes that gave the lie to the shuffle and the cracked voice. The detective nodded and said patronizingly,

'He sure is, ol'-timer.' Wheeler saw the sneer begin in the back of the eyes and was satisfied. 'Like to board him here,' Wheeler went on. 'Boss around?'

The old man's eyes flickered once, then he mumbled: 'Nope. He mostly leaves that kinda thing to me.' He was about to add something but then thought better of it.

'Well, if you're the foreman,' Wheeler said softly, giving the brush a final flick across Hassan's satiny rump, 'guess you'd better lead the way.'

Having finished with his pony, Wheeler made his way first to the eating-house indicated by the hotel clerk and from there to the office of the town marshal. Rolo was sitting in the office chair, his badge prominently displayed.

'Marshal in, deputy?' Wheeler asked diffidently. Rolo shook his head.

'Naw. Fatso's having supper. What d'you want?'

Wheeler shrugged. 'Looking for a man,' he offered. 'Name o' Collins. Land surveyor for the government.'

'Why might you be lookin' for 'im?' Rolo demanded sharply, too sharply to Wheeler's trained ears.

'Ain't no secret,' the detective whined, falling back into character. 'His wife ain't heard from him in a while. I was riding this way and she paid me to find 'im and give 'im a message.'

'What was the message?' Rolo demanded.

'Well, I guess that'd be my business,' Wheeler said nervously. 'Weren't nothin' agin the law, though.'

Surprisingly, Rolo nodded. 'Guess it is at that,' he said evenly. 'Your man was here. Vanished a coupla weeks ago. No one's seen hide nor hair of him since.'

'So you bin looking?' Wheeler asked mildly.

'Looked for a while,' Rollo admitted, 'but it's rugged country out there. Easy for a tenderfoot to get lost in.'

Wheeler shrugged and turned to go. 'Guess it wouldn't hurt to look around, though,' the detective offered as he reached for the wooden latch.

Rolo gave his visitor barely time to clear the sidewalk before he grabbed his hat and made his way by back alleys to the rear door of the Busted Dollar, bursting in to Rich Blagg's office and blurting:

'Fella just pulled in, lookin' fur Collins!'

'So? Anyone we know?' Blagg demanded, looking up.

'Looked like a cowboy riding the chuckline,' Rolo admitted. Nervously, the deputy glanced through Blagg's half-open door. Suddenly, he stiffened and leapt to the wall.

'That's him,' Rolo hissed, 'standing at the bar.'

Blagg rose from his desk, slowly shaking his head. He advanced to the door and gently closed it before turning a puzzled face to his employee.

'Why are you so jumpy?' Blagg demanded, 'He ain't gonna find Collins around here, is he? Unless, o' course,' he continued thoughtfully, 'there's something you ain't tellin' me, Rolo. I wouldn't like that,' the fat man snapped. 'I wouldn't like that at all!'

'No, it ain't nothing. Guess he just kinda spooked me,' Rolo admitted with a shamefaced grin. 'Didn't figure anyone'd come lookin'. Guess I better get back to the jail afore someone misses me.'

'Sure, you git along,' Blagg said suspiciously. He banged the bell on his desk and when a head appeared around the door, he snapped:

'Show him out and get Mona. Now.'

Rolo left by the back door, but the deputy didn't return to the jail immediately. Instead, he turned his steps to a tiny cantina on the outskirts of town where certain things were always available . . . at a price.

Blagg was sampling his own merchandise when there was a knock at the side door and the girl Mona slipped nervously into the room.

Without speaking, he rose and walked to the main door, opening it a bare crack. For a few moments, he carefully adjusted the view then, beckoning the girl, he whispered:

'D'you know that fella, Mona honey? The short one, in the black hat at the bar.' No reply was necessary. She took one look and jerked back into the room, hand flying to mouth.

'It's him,' she mouthed jerkily, 'the detective.' For a moment, she struggled against emotion, then blurted out: 'He can't see me, Rich. It'd . . .' That was as far as she got, because the fat man's hand slashed across her face, knocking her to the floor and starting a dribble of blood from the corner of her mouth. Blagg sneered down at her.

'Only thing you call me is "boss",' he whispered softly. 'And if he sees you, well, it'll be just too bad. For him and you.'

Carefully, he reached down, twined his hand into her hair and jerked her viciously to her knees. He reached into his pocket and produced an angular green bottle, set it on a nearby table and began slowly to unbutton his trousers.

'You want it, darlin?' he sneered. 'Well, you know what to do. Just open your mouth and . . . beg!'

Wheeler left the Busted Dollar just as twilight was falling, satisfied with the few small gleanings he had obtained, yet, at the same time, puzzled by the pattern that was slowly building up.

Occupied with his thoughts, he didn't notice the two shadowy figures that left the sheltering alleyway opposite the saloon and fell in a long gunshot behind him.

It wasn't long, though, before the sixth sense that comes to all men who ride dangerous trails prodded him. Without looking back, Wheeler paused, casually turning to light a smoke. There was a flurry of movement and the street was empty, but Wheeler had seen enough.

Mind racing, he paced heavily down the street. His next move depended on them. Probably they'd wait to catch him against the light of the hotel, where he'd be a sure target, silhouetted and blinded by the porch lamp, with a safe escape route down a nearby alley.

Ruefully, he looked up, mildly cursing the moonlight. He'd always been careful about moonlight since that night Chico had nearly finished him. Although . . . moonlight, of course, could work both ways.

Faintly, the two men following Wheeler heard a tinny melody drifting on the night air. Someone was whistling *Shenandoah.*

'It is just as I tol' you, *amigo.*' Pablo whispered to his good friend Jose as they watched the gringo turn into the box-and-barrel-filled alley that ran between the livery barn and its associated corral.

'This gringo, he iss a verra stupid one. Go there,' Pablo ordered, pointing to the middle of the alleyway. 'We will catch him between us.'

Carefully trying to avoid the garbage at his feet, Pablo began to creep along the wall of the livery barn but the accumulation of rubbish quickly forced him into the centre next to his friend. Moonlight was flooding the alley, brightly illuminating the space between the two killers and their intended victim. And that was all there was. Moonlight. Wheeler had vanished.

Slower on the uptake than his friend, Jose hissed:

'The gringo, Pablo, where is the . . .' He was interrupted by a familiar double click and a dry voice saying mildly:

'Get rid of the hardware, boys, and turn around with your hands up.'

Silhouetted against the moonlight, for a moment it looked as though they might obey. Pablo was actually lifting his gun clear of the holster when he seemed to stagger. He thrust Jose away from him and whirled, bringing up the pistol as he did so. He was barely half-way round, when there was a flat crack and a bullet lanced into his chest, throwing him backwards.

Caught off balance by his friend's push, Jose landed in the dirt, scrabbling for his gun. Coming to one knee, the Mexican fired into the shadows, only to hear his bullet whang off adobe. Before he could fire again, Wheeler's second shot caught him in the forehead, blowing his filthy sombrero and a goodly portion of his brains into the street behind him.

For some seconds the alley was quiet, then, as shouts came closer, there was a scraping and Wheeler rose stiffly from behind the barrel which had sheltered him.

Without a glance at his victims, he moved quickly towards the entrance of the alley, but suddenly the street was full of torches and men shouting. Even as he looked back, he saw lights behind and several men starting in his direction.

In desperation, he stumbled clumsily to the wall of the livery barn. In another minute the lights would reach him and then. . . . Without warning, he felt his arm gripped and a hard voice was saying:

'Quick, get in here!'

CHAPTER FOUR

Wheeler needed no second invitation. Awkwardly, he shifted through the door that had opened next to him and with his pistol held before him, he waited in the soft, horse-smelling darkness. There was another whiff of horse and his rescuer was leading him across a straw-covered floor. There was a feeling of space above him. A moment later, his arm was released, as the flare of a match blinded him.

By the time his eyes had adjusted, a lantern was swinging from its hook in the ceiling and the old livery man was carefully placing a worn Sharps Special into a makeshift rack in the corner.

'Sit down, mister,' the old man said without looking at Wheeler. 'Ain't no one gonna bother you here.' He glanced back as he approached the small stove that occupied one end of the little room. 'And you might want to put away that fancy contraption.'

For a moment, Wheeler's gaze swept the little room, then he carefully flipped down the Sibley back sight on the long-barrelled Colt and reached down to unscrew the canteen stock. The Colt was holstered and Wheeler was sitting in the least rickety chair in the place when the old man returned bearing two steaming cups.

Without bothering to ask, the old man uncorked a black bottle and added a good slug of clear liquid to each cup before taking the nearer one and settling back into a convenient chair. He took a long drink, apparently not noticing that Wheeler had left his own cup untasted. Without preamble, Wheeler asked softly:

'Why'd you do it?'

The old man shrugged. 'Can't stand a whipsaw,' he explained. 'Figured they had you cold and I bin lookin' fur an excuse to ventilate that slimy son of a whore Pablo for quite a piece now.'

'Don't like greasers, huh?' Wheeler asked mildly.

The old man shook his head. 'Nope. Pablo'd just lived too long, whatever colour he was,' he answered callously. 'Name's Hewitt,' he continued, 'Tex Hewitt, on account of that's where I was born. Most o' the know-nothin's round here call me "Horse-thief" because they think I am one.'

'Wilson,' Wheeler offered smoothly, 'Cord Wilson. And most people call me a son of a bitch 'cause they think I am one.'

Hewitt nodded. 'Bet they don't call you that to your face though,' he offered shrewdly. 'Coming down to cases, what you doing here Mr . . . Wilson?'

'Cowhand. Driftin'. Looking for a job,' Wheeler said quietly. Hewitt shook his head.

'No you ain't,' he contradicted easily.' A man is told by his tools and that,' he said pointing to the holstered revolver at Wheeler's side, 'ain't no shop-bought piece. That was made for a particular job for a man who knew

34

exactly what he wanted. What's it sighted to? Thirty yards?'

Wheeler sighed. 'About,' he admitted.

'And you can put nine shots out of ten into a six-inch group at that range, can't you?' Hewitt demanded.

Wheeler shrugged.

'So?' Hewitt demanded, 'Afore you decide how much you want to tell me,' the old man continued, spinning a flat disc of metal through the air towards Wheeler, 'take a look at this.'

'This' was a flat, tarnished badge. The star-in-circle badge of the Texas Rangers. For a second, Wheeler fingered the badge. Then, abruptly, he seemed to make up his mind.

'Guess it ain't no secret,' the detective admitted, 'and mebbe you can help me at that. I'm looking for a man. . . .'

When he'd finished, Wheeler sat back and took up his untasted cup.

Hewitt sighed. 'It sure ain't much of a story,' the old man offered, 'but Collins was here. And he was tellin' all the folks who'd listen that he was surveying for the railroad. Then, one mornin' he just wasn't around. Pony I'd hired him come in by hisself.' The old man spat accurately at a knot-hole. 'He weren't no surveyor, though,' Hewitt finished.

Wheeler nodded. 'Too much to ask how you know that?' he asked.

'Half his equipment was missing or wrong,' Hewitt answered. 'I seen that myself. And a pard o' mine, Shaky Charlie, was guiding him. Said he never took so much as a measurement. Spent all his time readin'.'

'Reading what?' Wheeler asked.

'Charlie said it looked like a letter,' Hewitt admitted, 'but he'd never let Charlie near enough to see it.'

'I'd like to talk to Charlie. If he's around,' Wheeler said.

'Can't be did,' Hewitt stated flatly, ' 'less'n you got a telegraph to the next world. They found Charlie with a knife in his guts down near Paesar's cantina. Never lived long enough to tell who done it. Knowing some-thing about the scum that hangs out in Paesar's, I was layin' for Pablo as a good even bet. Why, I never even thanked you for blowin' the bastard's light out!' he finished callously.

'When did Collins disappear?' Wheeler asked.

'I see where you're aheading.' Hewitt nodded. 'It were a coupla days afore we found ol' Charlie. Charlie was my pal, but his lip flapped a mite too easy,' he finished frankly.

Wheeler nodded, holding out his hand as he rose.

'I'm obliged to you.' he said simply.

Hewitt nodded. 'You can take it I'm on your side if you're in a tight spot,' the old man responded, while shaking hands. 'Charlie was a good friend.'

Wheeler had reached the door when the old man called:

'You might want to clean that piece afore you git back to your room. Never know who might be waiting,' he offered, indicating the cleaning-materials beneath a rickety bench. 'There's somethin' else just struck me,' he continued, as Wheeler drew his weapon and reached for the oil-can. 'How come there was fellas at both ends of the alley so quick after you shot them greasers?'

36

Wheeler nodded without showing any surprise. 'Thought about that myself,' Wheeler admitted, 'not to mention why in hell they tried to jump me in the first place.'

There was a surprise waiting for Wheeler when he returned to his hotel.

Or, at least, it should have been a surprise. . . .

No one was on the front desk when Wheeler entered the ramshackle building and, getting no response to his shouts, he leaned across the battered counter and hooked his key from the rack.

Silently, as was his habit, he moved noiselessly up the staircase and along the passage which lead to his room. Carefully, he bent down and examined the peeling woodwork. The tiny sliver of brown paper he had left jammed between the frame and door was gone. A rapid search of the floor didn't reveal it, so Wheeler knelt and pushed an ear to the keyhole. A moment later, he rose soundlessly and slipped the Smith & Wesson from its concealed holster. With a twisting wrench, he freed the door-handle and in the same movement pushed the door wide, stepping away from the opening as he did so. Only darkness lay beyond the opening.

'Whoever you are,' Wheeler grated, 'you better light that lamp pronto, 'cause one second from now, I start shooting.'

Abruptly, a match flared, filling the room with a lamp's yellow glow and a deep voice was saying:

'OK, stranger, come ahead, I ain't heeled.'

'You may not be, but what about the fella hiding behind the door?' Wheeler replied, without moving.

The first voice chuckled and subconsciously Wheeler noted that there was no fear in the heavy accents as the man said:

'Better come out, Rolo, I tol' you he wouldn't fall for it.'

Reluctantly, the big man edged into sight, only to freeze as Wheeler snapped:

'That's far enough, Deputy. Get rid o' the hawg-leg.'

White-faced and shaken, Rolo reached down and eased the weapon out of its cracked holster, then dropped it on to the floor.

'Get over there next to your friend,' the detective snapped, 'and you, Mister No Gun, keep your hands where I kin see 'em. You may be honest,' Wheeler concluded, advancing into the room, 'but if you are, your face is sure a liar.'

For a moment, anger flared in the eyes of the fat man in the broadcloth suit and fancy waistcoat, seated by the bed. Then his face cleared and spreading his hands, he said affably:

'Now, cowboy, is this any way to treat two people who come here to save you some trouble? Maybe quite a piece o' trouble. Now put away that gun and let's talk turkey.'

Carefully, Wheeler edged round until his back was to the inner wall. His gun still menaced the pair as he said:

'I'm right comfortable the way I am. First, who might you be?' He flicked the gun-barrel at the seated one as he spoke. The fat man nodded, but there might have been a shade of irritation in his tone as he said importantly:

'Fowler, Marv Fowler. I'm marshal o' this burg and I . . .'

'Make a habit o' rollin' people in their hotel rooms?' Wheeler demanded waspishly, before he remembered the character he was supposed to be playing and said more mildly. 'So what's that got to do with me?'

'We had two men killed here tonight, Mr . . . Wilson,' Fowler answered pompously. 'I want to ask you a few questions.' He licked his lips nervously before saying. 'Mind if I see your gun?'

With barely a moment's hesitation, Wheeler stepped forward and shoved the barrel of the Smith & Wesson against the fat man's porcine snout.

'I don't mind, Fatso,' he said softly, 'have a good smell. Bin fired recent, d'you think?'

Fowler didn't move and after a moment he shoved the gun to one side. His voice was steady as he said:

'Nope, it ain't. That your only sidearm?' Wheeler shook his head, mentally applauding the fat man's nerve.

'Got this as well,' Wheeler answered, tendering the long-barrelled Sibley Colt.

'Ain't been fired since the last time it was cleaned,' Fowler decided, 'but it's been cleaned plumb recent.' His look was a question and Wheeler shrugged diffidently as he holstered both of his weapons.

'Took a shot at a jack on the trail,' he admitted. 'Allus try and pull 'er through and oil 'er after she's been used.'

Fowler nodded, feeling that he might be gaining some advantage now the guns were away.

'My deppity tells me you come down here lookin' for someone,' Fowler began.

Wheeler shrugged, eyes on the floor.

'Ain't no secret,' he mumbled. 'Fella name of Collins. Wife said he's a surveyor for the railroad. Give me some money, asked me to give him a message, if'n I could find 'im.'

Fowler nodded. 'Well, let me save you some trouble, cowboy,' he began pompously. 'I saw your man Collins taking the trail to the railroad crossing, 'bout ten in the mornin', a coupla weeks ago. Even sent me a letter, asking me to send on his stuff, which I done.'

Despite his disbelief, Wheeler allowed his face to clear.

'Oh, well that's all right then, Marshal,' Wheeler offered, continuing as the marshal's face assumed a satisfied smile, 'if I could just see the letter, I'll telegraph his wife where she can find him.'

For an instant the smug mask dropped from Fowler's face and his fat lips drew back in a vicious snarl. Only for an instant, then the mask was back, but Wheeler had seen enough and he dropped a hand, letting it rest casually on the worn butt of the Smith & Wesson.

'Now look, Wheeler,' Fowler began almost reasonably, 'I ain't got the letter, but I'm telling you, Collins left here for El Paso.' The marshal rose and walked to the door, signalling his deputy out. He paused at the threshold and said good-humouredly:

'That shyster Collins ain't worth the trouble it'd take to find him. And it wouldn't be worth anybody getting theirselves into trouble with, say, the law, looking for 'im. Be seeing you.'

'Oh you can count on that, Marshal,' Wheeler said thoughtfully.

Not long afterwards, Tex Hewitt answered an insistent knocking at the side door of the livery stable, only to be confronted by a less than welcome visitor. The man wasted no time. Pushing past the old man, he halted under the battered hurricane lamp and began irritably:

'Why did you stick your nose in tonight? I had that bastard dead to rights! We could've had a nice neat hanging and no one the wiser!'

'Sure,' Hewitt acknowledged, 'only I don't never throw away a tool 'til it's no use to me.'

The other sneered.

'Mighty dangerous thing to monkey with,' he stated. 'Watch you don't cut yourself!'

'Oh I allus keep a good eye out, front and back,' came the waspish reply.

CHAPTER FIVE

Next morning saw Cord Wheeler up bright and early. His first call was to the Wells Fargo office.

'No sign o' your *amigo's* parcel at all,' replied the old man who ran the place. 'Sure you got the right address?'

'Sure,' Wheeler replied emphatically. 'He was certain it was sent but his wife never got it. Happened to ask the marshal about it but he says you never lose anything. Must be a good customer o' yours,' the detective remarked innocently.

The old man's chest swelled visibly.

'Can't say we never lose nothing,' he answered truthfully, 'but the marshal, he don't have much truck with freight. Ain't bin in here in a coon's age.' The old man shook his head doubtfully. 'Six, eight months mebbe.'

'Oh well.' Wheeler shrugged. 'Nowhere else in town he could've sent it from, I suppose?'

'Nope,' the old man replied firmly. 'Nearest depot is Wright's Crossing, and that's a fifty-mile ride across the desert.'

Wheeler's next stop was the telegraph office and last

of all with the feeling of a good morning's work completed, he stepped through the rickety batwings of the Busted Dollar, intent only upon a well-deserved glass of beer.

Across the street, in the telegraph office, Marv Fowler was picking up the sheaf of message-forms from behind the counter. Wheeler's lay on top and as the marshal laboriously read it, his habitual sneer relaxed into a satisfied smile. He tossed the stack of flimsies on to the desk and headed for the door.

Wheeler was finishing his first glass and lazily debating the advisability of a second when Fowler slid into the seat across the table from him. Without any preamble, the fat man said:

'I see you're still here.'

Wheeler grinned and replied lazily: 'Your brain must be working overtime, Marshal.'

Fowler glared back at him and snapped: 'Still figure to find 'im?'

Wheeler shook his head.

'Naw,' he admitted frankly, 'I'm betting he got as far as 'Paso and then figured to have him some fun. Mebbe he'll turn up, mebbe he won't, but it sure don't seem worth looking for him down here. I telegraphed and tol' his wife so.' That was true, but what Wheeler had failed to add was that the telegram in question was addressed to an El Paso post office and marked 'Left until called for'. He figured that would probably be sometime around doomsday.

Meanwhile, Fowler had relaxed visibly.

'So I guess you'll be leaving pretty soon, then?' the fat man asked.

Wheeler shook his head.

'Looks a likely spot for a little prospectin' and since I got a grub-stake, figured I might try my hand.'

'Others has thought the same as you but most of 'em barely make eatin' money,' Fowler sneered.

Wheeler nodded, then, on a chance, asked:

'Them hills north of town look likely. What d'you think?'

There might have been a tiny tightening around his mouth and a shade of tension in his figure, but Fowler's voice was steady as he jeered:

'Thought you knew something about mining! Them hills is the onlikeliest prospect you'd find anywhere!'

Wheeler nodded idly, mentally promising himself that north was the first direction he would ride in when he began his search for the fake surveyor who called himself Collins.

Next morning, just as dawn was lightening the sky and promising the town of Waco's Find another day full of heat and dust and flies, Wheeler gave his brush a last flick across Hassan's satiny rump and called to Hewitt, who was pushing hay into feed-bags.

'Need me a pack-horse, Horse-thief. Got one you can spare that won't lay down on me afore I make the foothills?'

The old man glared across at his companion and said with some disgust:

'Whyn't you go and play in the street with the rest o' the kids? Some of us has work to do.'

Wheeler hauled up on to a rung of the hay-loft ladder and having settled himself comfortably, said:

'Now, I'm serious, Horse-thief. Figger to do a mite o'

prospecting and I need more than my l'il horse kin carry by hisself. How 'bout that pretty black pony in the end stall?'

'Goddam it,' Hewitt snapped, 'you stay away from that killer. Can't you see I got the bastard chained and double-hobbled. If'n he got out o' that stall and I weren't here, he'd stomp you flat!'

Wheeler looked impressed.

'So I can't have the pretty black one.' He sighed. 'But you must have a pack-pony I can use. What about the one Collins rode?'

'Oh, him.' Hewitt shrugged disparagingly. 'Sure, you kin borry him. It's the little pinto, old Rat-tail.'

Wheeler nodded his thanks, asking casually as he turned towards the animal in question:

'Suppose Collins never left any of his stuff here?'

Hewitt shrugged again and, for once, Wheeler missed the keen, malevolent glance thrown in his direction.

'Think his saddle-bag may be in the tack-room. Opposite Thunderhead's stall, if you're interested,' Hewitt offered, gesturing vaguely.

'Naw, not me,' Wheeler answered with a head shake. 'His wife can pay someone else to go look in 'Paso. By the way,' Wheeler continued innocently, 'she said he was missing a finger. That right?'

'Sure,' Hewitt said carefully,' on his right hand.'

'Camp-fire job?' Wheeler asked.

Hewitt shook his head. 'Naw, It looked pretty neat. Said he got frostbit and some travellin' medico did it for him. For someone who ain't interested in this *hombre*, you sure are all of a sudden,' the old man grumbled.

45

Wheeler shrugged.

'No, just curious about that finger. How 'bout some coffee?' he suggested.

Hewitt glared back at him.

'You should know where the fixings are by now!' the old man snapped. 'And I take plenty o' sugar in mine!'

Wheeler grinned and headed for the door. At least now he knew the real identity of the man calling himself Collins.

Having given Hassan all the currying that even that good tempered pony could endure, and being requested impolitely by Hewitt to bother someone else, Wheeler wandered casually down to the town's tiny general store. Small it might have been but, while making a few necessary purchases for his trip into the hills, Wheeler was surprised to find it remarkably well-stocked. He said as much to the brisk little man, clearly the owner, who gave his name as Ed Harris.

'I sure need to have aplenty of everything,' the peppery little man agreed, taking Wheeler's prof-fered bill. 'We may not look like much but there's a coupla big ranches use us for supplies and there's talk that the railroad's thinkin' of running a spur down here, for cattle- shipping. Yes sir,' the storekeeper finished enthusiastically. 'Waco's Find sure looks set to boom.'

'Sure seems a nice quiet little town now,' Wheeler offered.

'Quiet!' Harris snapped. 'Well, I guess it is these days, but if'n you'd come through five years ago, you would-n't have said so! Don't you know this is where Levi

Levinson and his boys was finally caught?' Wheeler appeared suitably impressed.

'Don't say,' he answered with an impressed whistle.' They was all killed, weren't they?' The little man shook his head.

'No sir. Old Levi and three of his boys was took up to El Paso tried and hung in front of the court house there. Town marshal, Marshal Fowler took 'em there himself. Stayed for the trial, too. Said he wanted to see justice done. Guess that tells you what sort of man we got as town marshal!'

Wheeler, who had his own ideas about the sort of man Fowler was, nodded again and said:

'Guess they musta found a heap o' coin on the old man.'

Harris gave a snort of derision.

'Not a cent!' the little man said. He lowered his voice and continued. 'Lot of folk think all their loot – ten years worth o' robberies – is cached in the hills. Everybody knew old Levi wouldn't pay for nothin' he could steal. So I guess he never paid for nothing!'

Harris laughed, then became thoughtful. 'Funny thing though,' he added, 'I remember now, that at the time lot of folks thought it was funny they was anywhere near a bank. I mean, they had travellin' money, grub, cartridges and a coupla spare horses. I seen it all when they was brung in. So why chance robbing a bank? Just plain greedy I guess.'

Wheeler nodded thoughtfully.

'I guess so,' he agreed.

It was almost full dark when Wheeler eased open the door of the livery stable and shuffled clumsily inside carrying his purchases. He had purposely delayed his return until the time the old man habitually left for his dinner and he gave a brief grunt of satisfaction on finding the building deserted.

A single kerosene-lamp swinging overhead filled the stable with shadows as Wheeler dropped his packages and moved carefully up to the tack-room which Hewitt had said contained Collins's saddle-bags. They might easily hold nothing of interest but knowing now who Collins really was, Wheeler felt the bags had to be worth searching.

Noiselessly, he moved past the patiently chewing lines of horses, until he was level with Thunderhead's stall. The big black tossed his head and bared his teeth, lunging angrily against his tether, while slamming both hind hoofs viciously into the boards at the rear of his stall. Wheeler shifted carefully away from him, some little worm of cowboy instinct nagging at the back of his mind. Something wasn't right but he dismissed the thought as he entered the saddle store.

What Hewitt had grandly called the tack-room was in fact a big disused stall, opposite the one occupied by Thunderhead, where horse owners could leave their gear. Wheeler swiftly surveyed the saddles and bridles until he found what he was looking for.

Collins's saddle-bags were the only ones visible. They were old and worn and Wheeler had just undone the first buckle when suddenly the sounds from Thunderhead's stall took on a new and ominous note. The stallion was no longer tearing at the headstall. For a brief moment, nothing stirred, then Wheeler was snatching at a gun as the head of the fighting-mad black lunged at him, the savage animal's teeth snapping shut in the space where Wheeler's arm had been a mere instant before.

With barely a pause, the stallion drew back, rearing and biting but, in that instant, Wheeler loosed his gun butt as though it were red-hot and, sweeping up a nearby saddle, flung it, muscles cracking, full in the face of the fighting-mad stud. The saddle struck the big black full on the chest, stopping him hardly long enough for Wheeler to swarm up the adjacent wood-work, with the intention of dropping into the next stall. Swiftly, the detective swung one leg across the worn paling but, disastrously, his heel caught and he was pitched headlong into straw, his knee twisting under him.

Desperately, he tried to rise but the knee twinged and buckled as the maddened stallion jerked back-wards, red-rimmed eyes glaring around in search of his victim.

Wheeler lay very still in the shadows as the huge animal moved away, stamping and tossing his head, clearly scenting the man but unable to detect the prone figure lying so close. Carefully, Wheeler gathered his legs silently under him. He had one chance.

If he could make the ladder to the hay-loft, he was safe until either Hewitt returned or he could drop out of the second-storey window. Desperately cautious, freezing at the least sound, he rose to his feet and edged out of the shadows and round the corner of the stall.

Cautiously, he began to limp heavily towards the ladder, eyes glued to the head-tossing stallion who stamped and kicked aimlessly under the solitary, swinging hurricane-lamp. Deadly though his position was, still some part of Wheeler's mind noted the horse's odd behaviour and wondered at it.

His luck held until he was barely half-way to the ladder. Then his foot clicked against a discarded piece of gear hidden in the straw-covered floor. In the silence, it sounded loud as a gunshot and Thunderhead whirled madly in response.

For a moment the black seemed unsure, as if unable to focus on the hobbling Wheeler and the detective managed to make two stumbling paces further, barely within hand-reach of the ladder, when a terrifying scream split the air and Wheeler heard the thunder of hoofs behind him.

Desperately, he clawed at the rungs but was barely half-way to the top when savage teeth snapped inches from his face and a pair of rock-hard hoofs smashed into the ladder, knocking Wheeler to the dust-and-straw-covered floor.

For a long moment, Wheeler lay on his back, partially stunned and desperately shaking his head to clear it. His clouded vision allowed him to see only the vague black shape of Thunderhead bearing down on him and he braced himself for the impact of the razor-sharp hoofs. Molly, he thought inconsequentially, is gonna be really annoyed about this.

CHAPTER SIX

Even as the detective steeled himself for the slashing, tearing impact, the stallion screamed in sudden rage and the black shape in his blurred vision instantly disappeared.

As his eyes slowly began to clear, Wheeler saw that, miraculously, a rope had appeared around the neck of the stallion and Tex Hewitt was dragging the horse backwards across the littered floor.

Without hesitation, Wheeler stumbled to his feet and, seconds later, he was out of the nearby side-door, breathing the sweet night air and wondering why he hadn't been smashed to jam under Thunderhead's hoofs.

Some minutes passed before Hewitt slammed through the main door, threw his rope to the floor and rasped:

'I tol' you not to monkey with that killer! Goddammit, why in hell d'you cut 'im loose for?'

'Cut 'im loose?' Wheeler echoed.' I was stowing some gear in there when he jumped me! I was never anywhere near him!

With a sneer the old man held up a length of halter-line and a plaited hobble.

'Then how d'you explain that?' he asked simply. 'That' was the clean-cut end of the leather halter.

Wheeler shrugged and his grin was icy as he said softly:

'Looks like mebbe somebody don't want me to find our friend Collins after all.' Then he chuckled and Hewitt shivered because there was no joy or pleasure at all in the sound.

'Come to think about it, being stove up by a hoss is maybe just what I need right now,' Wheeler muttered thoughtfully.

It was a sad little procession that staggered over to the hotel that night. Wheeler lay clutching his side on a stretcher supported by two Mexicans, while Hewitt followed behind lugging the old bag he always took on his horse-doctoring chores.

'Goddammit, take it easy up them steps, you ham-fisted pair of greaser bastards,' Wheeler swore as the stretcher pole jerked against an inconvenient veranda-post. Hewitt was beside him, clucking and shushing as the patient was carefully transported to his room.

'Ain't no point thinkin' o' moving him,' Hewitt remarked to Rolo, who had happened to amble by. 'That bastard stallion larruped 'im in the ribs. I'm guessing he's got a coupla days of laying still afore he heads into them hills.'

The deputy nodded, hiding a sneer of satisfaction behind his hand, before hurrying off.

Rich Blagg was unconcerned when Rolo brought him the news.

'Can't see it makes no difference to us,' the fat saloon keeper offered. 'All the same,' he added thoughtfully, 'if he ain't gonna be around for a coupla days, you might look over his horse and fixings, just to make sure he don't know nothin' that we oughta.'

Never one to let the grass grow under his boots, Rolo returned to Hewitt's livery stable as soon as he left Blagg's office. The battered lamp was still swinging from a convenient roof-beam as he made his way past the stall of the exhausted and still twitchy Thunderhead and entered the area marked off for horse-furniture.

Carelessly, Rolo kicked aside a couple of saddles before stooping towards the one he wanted.

'Now where's that bastard Wheeler keep his coin,' he rumbled. Surprisingly, a voice behind him snapped,

'Right here!'

Slow and fat Rolo may have been but there was nothing wrong with his instincts. Almost before the words were out of his assailant's mouth, he had thrust himself away from the saddle and was swinging in a driving turn towards the man.

He never made it. Something smashed into the side of his head and deposited him at full length on the floor, stunned and barely conscious. He tried to rise but the shadowy figure above him struck expertly and Rolo went to sleep for a very long time.

For a moment there was silence and then Hewitt's voice said reasonably,

'Ain't much on that fair fight business, are ye?' There was a derisive snort and the sound of something heavy dropping to the floor as Wheeler approached his victim. He bent and examined the fat man briefly.

'Well he'll live anyways,' he said, 'and no, I ain't got no time for "fair fights".' The last two words were a sneer as Wheeler added, 'To me, a fair fight is one I win, Horse-thief, any way I can. Only reason I didn't shoot the bastard was 'cause o' the noise,' he finished insincerely.

'You don't believe that any more'n I do,' Hewitt grunted, 'Come on,' the old man added, 'We got ponies to pack.'

The nature and timing of a cowboy's work means that he more often than not saddles his pony in the darkness. It didn't take Wheeler and his companion long to swing the gear aboard Hassan and the little pinto Hewitt called Rat-tail. Despite his derisory name, the little gelding was quiet and well trained and he sighed and huffed contentedly as Wheeler ran a knowing hand over his hard little flank. Wheeler's satisfied nod was lost in the darkness as he said,

'Good l'il pony, Hoss-thief.'

'Sure,' the old man agreed. 'He won't let you down.'

Quietly, Wheeler swung aboard Hassan and kneed him around, without bothering to do more than knot the reins across the saddle horn in front of him, gathering the little pinto's lines as he did so. Without needing to be told, Hewitt eased one of the big doors open and Wheeler said as he passed:

'Keep everybody out o' my room, Hoss-thief. Tell 'em – oh anything you figure. If I ain't back in a week, come and bury what's left.' With that cheerful valediction, Wheeler nudged his pony and Hassan loped easily into the night.

For a moment Hewitt looked after him, then the old

man shrugged and spat in the dust.

'Sure a shame,' he mumbled. 'I'm figgering that boy's straight.'

Wheeler was too wise in the ways of the desert country to be careless about his animals' welfare. Consequently, he waited only to be well clear of town before stopping and picketing both of them on some reasonable grass. His ponies taken care of, he rolled into a blanket and slept until dawn was beginning to spread its pearly fingers across the western sky. Eschewing breakfast, he was in the saddle and pushing steadily northwards before full daylight, avoiding the plain-trails and sticking to a system of draws and little coulees that led him steadily towards the mountains, while he searched the ground on either side.

He had been riding for nearly two hours and the dew was long gone from the grass when he found what he wanted.

He pulled Hassan gently to a halt, and examined the area of smooth sand before dismounting and leading Rat-tail carefully across it. He tied the little gelding securely some distance from the patch and then moved carefully back to it, examining the pony's hoof-prints as he did so. Finally satisfied that he could identify the little gelding's tracks if he saw them again, Wheeler carefully smoothed the sand and having whistled Hassan to him, mounted and headed both animals north and back towards the main trail.

His luck proved to be in almost immediately, because he cut the pinto's trail in a little flood-washed arroyo, luckily protected from the scouring wind.

Being careful not to disturb the tracks, Wheeler

backed Hassan out of the depression, picketed both his animals out of sight, then moved back to the undisturbed trail. Carefully staying on the rocky scree that lined the floor of the arroyo, Wheeler squatted comfortably and began his study of the story written in the dust before him.

The trail was old, made at least a month previously and as Wheeler studied the shallow impressions, a faint line, which became a deepening furrow appeared on his brow. Once he got up and moved carefully to the other end of the arroyo and squatted patiently, studying his story from that new angle. On the face of it, it seemed plain enough.

Three horses had entered the arroyo, Indian file, one behind the other. One of the ponies had been Rattail and of the others, one had been similar in size to the tough little pinto, and the other, a mare, had been much larger. They'd all been ridden and no rider had stopped or dismounted and no horse had left even a hair from which its colour might be told. So far, so good. Except. . . .

When a tenderfoot trails a pony or a man he usually congratulates himself upon being able to see a footprint. The expert reaches far beyond this. He observes all the little idiosyncrasies which go into the placement of foot or hoof and reads therein much that a newcomer misses. Wheeler's education in tracking had been extensive and thorough and there was something about the trail left by the pinto that was wrong. Patiently, he shifted to a new position, re-examining the tracks as he went.

An hour later, he found it. It was only a little thing,

easy to miss in that vastness of sand and dust. Plain now, on the trail, Wheeler saw where the second horse had shied, perhaps only at a waving sagebrush. Following behind, Rat-tail had plainly staggered backwards also, for no apparent reason. Wheeler grunted with satisfaction.

'The l'il fella was being led,' he decided as he walked back to the ponies. 'And that means Collins was, too.'

Late afternoon found Wheeler hot upon the month-old trail, when suddenly the tracks disappeared as though they had never been. He was opposite the entrance to a little draw, similar to several he'd seen that day and, anxious not to be forced to do his chores in darkness, he decided to camp for the night. He felt no concern about the disappearance of the tracks. After all, they were a month old and whoever he was following was unlikely to try getting behind him in the dark.

His fire was well alight and the coffee-pot just beginning to bubble as Wheeler removed the feed-bag from Hassan's ears. Carefully placing the grain-filled sack against his saddle, he whistled shortly and began to walk towards an area of sagebrush and bunch-grass that seemed to offer good grazing, the well-trained Hassan following contentedly behind.

Suddenly, the little grey gave a whiffling snort and jerked aside, eye-whites showing clear around the socket. Wheeler looked back in exasperation.

'Quit your play-acting, you old fool . . .' he began, then stopped abruptly. The tough little grey's eyes were wide with fear and Wheeler, whose trust in his four-footed partner's instincts was absolute, turned carefully and made his way back to where the little grey stood, braced and trembling. Slowly, Wheeler backed him away from the spot.

For a few moments he patted and caressed, then slowly led the little half-Arab forward. Instantly, Hassan balked and jerked his head back. Repeating the experiment with Rat-tail yielded the same result and it was with some satisfaction that Wheeler rolled into his blankets that night, carefully keeping his bed-roll clear of the spot which the animals found so distasteful.

Sun-up found Wheeler breakfasted and, armed with a shovel, he began to investigate the cause of the previous night's disturbance. In a few minutes, he had dug away the top layer of sand, only to encounter a second layer, which consisted of large stones loosely piled. Swiftly, Wheeler cleared sand from the largest of these flattish slabs and, grunting with effort, he forced the blade of the shovel under a convenient side and levered the slab away. The rest of the stones soon followed, exposing another layer of sand. This time, the blade of the shovel lanced in easily and, with a grimace of distaste, Wheeler began to spoon the sand out, exposing a long sheath of sun-dried brown leather as he did so. At last he stood back. In the hole he had made there lay a battered, high-heeled cowboy boot, complete with leg. Or rather what was left of the leg.

Only thing was, Wheeler admitted to himself, as he moved around and began to dig where he calculated the body's head to be, it was a dollar to a gold watch that the man who called himself Collins had never worn such an article in his life.

CHAPTER SEVEN

It was the beginning of what looked like a profitable evening in the Busted Dollar and Rich Blagg was feeling expansive. At least, that seemed to be the case from where Rolo sat, enjoying a glass of Blagg's good stock and a better than reasonable cigar.

'Gonna clean up around here when the railroad comes through,' Blagg continued, 'an' I don't aim to forget my friends! How'd you figure the marshal's job'd sit with you?'

Rolo grimaced. 'Fine,' he admitted, 'so long as somebody else tells Fowler.' Rolo leaned forward and went on earnestly: 'You don't know him like I do, Rich. He ain't stupid, not by a long sight and it wouldn't pay to sell him short!'

'Scared?' Blagg sneered.

Rolo nodded shortly. 'Man who don't know his limits is a fool. Usually a dead fool,' he rumbled. Blagg waved aside his companion's objections.

'Fowler ain't worrying me near as much as someone else,' Blagg admitted. Rolo looked puzzled and Blagg said simply: 'Mona. I think she's gettin' . . . unreliable.'

The deputy gave a piglike grunt of understanding, then asked:

'Who d'you want me to use?'

Blagg thought a moment. 'Make it Pedro,' he said. Might be as well to have somethin' on that slippery little greaser bastard.'

Things hadn't been exactly smooth for Mona since her trip to El Paso. She'd noted a decided cooling in Blagg's response to her and while she welcomed it as a relief from his disgusting body and ludicrous demands, she knew it didn't bode well for the future. Lately, when her opium-fuelled craving became too much to bear, she had taken to roaming Waco's darkened side-streets. With Wheeler still in town, it had been dangerous and she knew if Blagg had ever caught her she would not have waited long for death but now she was past caring and as the aching in her body grew, she roamed further afield, desperate to still the craving that racked her.

She'd left the saloon early that night, meaning only to go a little way, but darkness had caught her unawares and now she hurried onwards, desperate to be back and safe in the unlikely event that Blagg would demand her services that evening.

She was passing the darkened alleyway next to Hewitt's livery when she heard her name softly called. Slowly, she advanced into the lightless opening and Pedro, crouched and waiting in the shadow of the building, silently slipped the razor-sharp blade from its beadwork sheath. This was easy. As the woman came into the alley, he would reach up, grab her hair, push back the head and a single stroke in the throat would

61

finish it. It was a shame that there could be no play, but the *señor* deputy had been clear. Any mistakes were liable to be personally fatal. For Pedro.

Closer, just a little closer, now, *señorita. Bueno.* But as Pedro reached forward, his sombrero was suddenly slapped over his face and he was thrust backwards, to land sprawling in the dust, still, fortunately, clutching his knife, while an *Americano* voice said softly:

'Now, *amigo*, that ain't no way to treat a lady.'

Mad with rage, Pedro swept the hat from his face, lunged to his feet and launched a savage thrust at the sneering figure before him. But the knife cut only empty air and as Pedro stumbled past, he felt a faint breath of air before a red-hot fire swept the length of his face.

Involuntarily, the would-be killer's hand leapt to his cheek and what he felt caused a rapid sobering. His opponent, whoever he was, had neatly laid his face open, just as though he had used a surgeon's knife. Pedro paused, eyes fixed on the crouched figure before him. He spared one rapid glance at the terrified woman, huddled back against the wall, then his attention flicked back to his opponent.

Cautiously, the Mexican moved right, following his knife. Suddenly he appeared to drop to his knees, and then he was driving in, swinging the wicked blade under the other's guard, driving towards the knife-fighter's favourite target, the belly. But, unbelievably, his opponent wasn't there and fear surged through the Mexican as he felt his wrist trapped in an iron grip.

Then, suddenly, there was pain, pain flaming through his entire arm, causing him to drop his blade and stagger back as the blood spouted from a gash which had opened his forearm to the bone.

For a moment, Pedro stood still, simply glaring his fear and hatred. Then he turned and ran.

Knife still in hand, the man glared after his victim, until, apparently satisfied that he was gone for good, he turned back to the woman. Moonlight flickered briefly across his face. Looking up at her saviour, Mona managed a weak grin.

'Why, Mr Wheeler, fancy seeing you here,' she said nervously, then she fainted right away.

'Firstly, his name ain't and never was Collins,' Cord Wheeler stated flatly.

After the girl had recovered from her faint, Wheeler had managed to get her up the back stairs of the old hotel and into his room. Unfortunately, neither of them had seen the figure in the shadows, a figure who clutched an arm from which blood dripped in a steady trickle and whose hate-filled glare had followed them as they entered the little hotel.

From her seat in the room's only reasonably comfortable chair, the girl shrugged and said cautiously:

'I don't know nothin' about that. I just done what Ri . . . what I was told.'

Wheeler nodded shortly, apparently not noticing her slip.

'I guess there ain't no real reason you should know,' he replied mildly, 'Collins's real name was Royston. Folks called him Three-finger Jack on account of he lost the little finger of his right hand after he cut it on a can o' bad oysters and it got infected. It was what put me on to this whole business in the first place,' Wheeler continued. 'I remembered that ol' Jack had been Levinson's lawyer. In fact, he got put in the pen soon after for stealin' his clients' money. Run as far as New Orleans afore they caught him.' Wheeler sighed, painfully dragging his mind from the past.

'Some folks claimed,' he continued, 'that Royston was the contact who gave Levinson and his boys the inside dope they needed to pull their biggest jobs. And them same folks said that Royston knew where Levinson had hidden the loot.' Wheeler finished significantly.

'But I still don't understand,' Mona said. 'How did you know Collins was Royston?'

'Pretty easy really,' Wheeler assured her. 'Man works on the range, cowboy, skinner, railroad man, it ain't uncommon to lose a finger or even a hand or sichlike, But it ain't often an office man like a surveyor gets in the way of something that'll injure him like that. Soon as you told me about the finger I got suspicious. And then when you said he'd gone missing in Waco's Find, I was almost sure it had to be Royston.'

'Why?' Mona demanded.

Wheeler spread his hands. 'Because this was the li'l piss-ant town that Levinson and his boys were caught in. A three-fingered man matching Royston's description in Waco's Find was too much of a coincidence for me to pass up,' he said simply.

'And you're certain that Collins is Royston?' Mona asked. After Wheeler had nodded slowly, she continued. 'Well, it seems like you've wasted your time, Mister Clever Detective. Collins has been gone from here for weeks. How d'you know he ain't in 'Paso or even San Francisco, spending that coin and laughin' at you?'

'I didn't,' Wheeler admitted, 'until two days ago, when I found him. Dead,' he added before the girl could speak. 'And don't ask me how he died, 'cause I've seen comfortabler corpses left by the Apaches.' When the white-faced girl made no attempt to speak, Wheeler resumed:

'Funny thing was, though, he weren't alone. Had another fella, cowboy, buried with 'im. The other fella'd been plugged with something that weren't a Colt. Something small,' he added.

Wheeler studied the girl without speaking for some moments.

'Thing is, Miz Mona,' he resumed, 'Collins must have had some reason for being down here. And if, like I figure, it was Levinson's cache, he must have had a map or directions. Now,' he grimaced with distaste. 'I know there was nothin' like that on the body 'cause I looked. And I figure he was too smart to carry it around with him, in case he was robbed. So that only leaves his gear in the hotel, which they got behind the desk. But before we get any further along,' Wheeler offered, 'I'd kinda like to know where you fit into this.'

Mona shrugged. 'Like I told you,' she said simply, 'it was just a job.' Briefly, she described the events of that morning in Rich Blagg's office. When she had finished, Wheeler said:

'So your friend Blagg wanted Collins found. Does he ever carry a gun?'

Mona shook her head. 'Nope,' she said firmly, 'if he wants someone killed, he hires it done. I mean,' she corrected herself hastily, 'Rolo does.'

'The deputy marshal?' Wheeler demanded, and when the girl nodded, he said, 'He sports a .44 Colt Frontier but I guess a man can own more'n one gun. Question is now,' Wheeler went on, 'how to get a look at Collins's gear?'

'I may be able to help you there,' Mona offered, jerking her head nervously as the laudanum demons began to nip at her, 'for a . . . ah . . . consideration. And as long as you can keep Rolo away from me.' She paused, considering, then a slow smile spread across her face as she asked:

'You got mebbe a piece a paper an' a pencil?' Briefly, the muscles of her face arched. 'And for Chrissake get me a drink!' she snapped.

The subject of Wheeler's and Mona's discussion had, at that moment, something other than laudanum-addicted whores on his mind. Rolo was having to own to another failure and the look in Rich Blagg's eye was making him feel distinctly uncomfortable.

'And you say Pedro just got back?' Blagg demanded.

'Just this minute,' Rolo agreed nervously. 'Arm's all cut up and he's bleeding like a stuck pig.'

'And what's his story?' the saloonkeeper rasped.

Rolo shrugged. 'Claims he was about to knife the girl when this fella jumped him. Says he used a knife better'n Jim Bowie. Cut Pedro up like he was some kid and then took the girl to the hotel.'

'Pedro recognize 'im?' Blagg snapped.

'Nope,' Rolo admitted. 'But there's only one stranger stayin' at that flea-bag. You want me to finish the job, boss?' Rolo asked nervously.

'Yes,' Blagg decided, after a moment's thought, 'but leave the detective. He may be hanging around for a reason and if he's got something on Collins, we want to know.'

Rolo nodded and turned to go. At the door, he turned and asked:

'What about Pedro, boss?'

Blagg looked through him for a moment.

'One armed greaser ain't no more use than a broken-legged horse, is he,' Blagg demanded softly.

Rolo nodded and closed the door after him. Plainly, the boss was in no forgiving mood tonight. Rolo sneered. Blagg was a fool if he wanted to discard a tool with a hatred as sharp as Pedro's.

Rolo found the little Mexican in a filthy back room, and, having ascertained that the damage to his arm was not as great as both men had first thought, Rolo slapped his companion on the back.

'This is sure your lucky day,' he offered.

The Mexican shrugged. 'Don' seem like it from here!' he snapped, nursing the injured arm.

'Oh, believe me, it is,' Rolo stated, seating himself comfortably. 'Boss just told me to shoot you, like you was a broken-legged horse.' He watched the consternation in the greaser's eyes and when he was sure the man was just frightened enough, Rolo said easily:

'But I ain't like him. I don't just get rid of people who bin useful to me.' Briefly, he fumbled in a pocket, before drawing out a couple of bills and shoving them into the Mexican's hand.

'Got somewheres you kin hide out?' Rolo demanded

and when the Mexican had muttered his answer, the deputy continued:

'Good. You get out now by the back way and let me know where you are. We ain't finished with Mr Rich Blagg, Pedro, not by a long way but I'm gonna need you to help me swing it.'

'Jus' say de word, *señor* and he is . . .' the flickering hand-gesture was unmistakable and Rolo nodded.

'I'll keep it in mind,' he assured the other. 'Now git.'

He watched as his companion slipped across the lightless back lot, heading towards the little Mexican quarter of Waco's Find, before leaving in the opposite direction himself.

Mebbe you ain't quite as clever as you thought, you fat bastard, Rolo thought, as he settled himself comfortably in the shadows opposite the hotel. Killed by a greaser and your 'business partner' inherits the whole thing. Now, wouldn't that be a shame? And nobody could prove a thing.

Suddenly, he stiffened and an oath leapt from his lips. What in hell was she doing there?

CHAPTER EIGHT

The 'she' in question was Mona, who was sauntering along the sidewalk outside the hotel as though she had nothing on her mind except a more or less innocent evening's entertainment. Certainly, she didn't look as though someone had tried to cut her throat less than an hour ago. Rolo cursed again.

'Damn a whore,' he muttered. 'Harder to kill than a Mimbrenos Apache.'

Mona might not have agreed with him as she paused in the hotel doorway and withdrew a reeking envelope from her inadequate reticule. Waving it idly in front of her face she sauntered into the ramshackle lobby.

Looking up from the week-old newspaper that had been occupying his attention, the little hotel clerk sighed and snapped:

'No whores in here. Go pedal your ass some other place!'

Mona appeared not to hear as she continued her slow gliding walk, languidly inspecting the scabby walls and peeling paintwork as she did so. She halted in front of the desk, still idly waving the letter and after a last look round, said waspishly:

'I can see how a fancy place like this would need to pertect its reputation from someone like me.'

The little clerk opened his mouth but Mona waved him to silence.

'Don't get your pants in a tangle, Jackie,' she reassured him. 'I ain't here on that sorta business.' She waved the letter suggestively. 'Friend o' mine seen you in the Dollar the other night,' she continued, winking lasciviously. 'She's particular about the gentleman friends she entertains and she asked me to give you this.' She waved the letter under his nose. Wheeler, who was waiting out of sight on the first landing, caught a faint whiff that almost made him gag.

Jackie had no such misgiving. He snatched the letter and tore it open with shaking hands. Mona waited patiently while his finger traced the scribbled words, mouthing silently to himself. After a little, he looked up.

'She wants to meet me,' he stammered, 'in the saloon. But she don't say who she is.' Vaguely, he looked around, then gestured despairingly. 'And I can't leave this goddamn place!'

'Hell,' Mona shrugged 'Don't worry about that. I'll watch the place for you.' Seeing the dubious look on his face, she added, 'What are you worried about, stupid? Ain't nothin' I can steal, is there?'

Jackie thought as rapidly as his limited intellectual processes would allow. She was certainly right about there being nothing worth stealing. And the letter . . . it might, after all, be from that little greaser, Conchita, the one he'd been trying to pluck up courage to try for ever since he'd seen her in Blagg's. OK, so she was a whore, but. . . . Abruptly, he made up his mind.

'Just check the keys against the book,' he ordered. 'I'll be back . . . when I. . . .'

Mona nodded.

'Sure, I know,' she offered crudely. 'You'll come when you can.'

The little man was barely out of the door before the watcher, hidden in the shadows across the street, saw Wheeler slip silently down the stairs. The lean detective moved behind the desk.

'How long d'you reckon he'll be?' Wheeler demanded. Mona looked at the desk clock.

'Conchita don't usually come down 'til late,' she mused, 'and by the time the little slut's explained to poor ol' Jackie that there ain't no way he's ever gonna be one o' her regulars . . . I guess we got at least an hour.'

Wheeler nodded. 'Watch the front,' he ordered softly. 'Stall anyone who ain't the clerk and if you see him comin' back afore I'm finished, knock on the wall.'

Without waiting for an acknowledgement, Wheeler moved silently through the doorway behind the desk. Swiftly, he searched through the place and had all but given up in despair when he stumbled upon the little storeroom he was looking for. Only to find it locked.

It took him several more of his precious minutes to ease the lock open so that his entry was undetectable and even then the jumble of gear that presented itself to him seemed impossible to penetrate.

More precious minutes ticked by and even

Wheeler's iron nerve was feeling the strain, when he finally found a single, battered carpet-bag with a tattered label bearing Collins's name. Its contents were hardly world-shaking. A clean shirt, some unimportant letters, and an assortment of cheap bric-à-brac. Only one thing seemed out of place. It was a finely polished writing-case, about twelve inches long and half as broad. It was heavy and Wheeler was just about to open it when a hiss from the doorway stopped him.

'It's Jackie,' she whispered from the region of the floor, 'he's back and he ain't happy!'

Noiselessly, Wheeler slipped the writing-case into a pocket of his duster coat. It was the work of seconds to close and relock the storeroom door, then he was clasping the frightened girl by the hand and pulling her soundlessly across the cluttered living-room and into the tiny kitchen.

They had barely time enough. Wheeler had only just managed to close the rickety door before they heard the slam of the counter and the little clerk's monotonous cursing. Wheeler grinned in the darkness and whispered:

'Ain't got much imagination, has he?' He listened for a moment, then continued, 'And I'd say you ain't his favourite person. Come on,' he finished, silently shifting towards the rear door.

Obediently, Mona followed him. Momentarily, his head was silhouetted against the moonlit window, then she heard a tiny grunt of effort as he threw his weight against the door-handle. But nothing moved and her anxiety was filling the dark with demons when she felt a light touch on her arm and Wheeler's voice was breathing in her ear.

'Son of a bitch has fixed the lock,' he whispered. 'I can't open it, so . . . we'll have to get out through the front.'

Urgently, he tugged her arm and together they moved next to the kitchen's inner door. Carefully, Wheeler placed his ear against the door. For what seemed like an eternity to the frightened girl, he listened in silence, then he whispered:

'Sounds like he's still out front. See if that stove's alight, will you? I've mebbe got me an idea.'

To say that Jackie was annoyed would have been something of an understatement. The little hotel clerk had all but exhausted his stock of bad words on the little whore Conchita, who, to add insult to the raucous indignity of her refusal, had had Big Joe, the bouncer at the Busted Dollar, throw him unceremoniously into the street. His rage had become incandescent upon returning to the hotel, when he found the desk unoccupied and the door open to all and sundry.

His cursing had finally dwindled to a dissatisfied muttering when his ample nostrils picked up a peculiar and worrying smell. Moving with increasing rapidity, as the stink grew stronger, Jackie passed swiftly into the back room. Plainly the smell was coming from the kitchen. Paying no attention to anything else, the little man jerked open the door, to find the cluttered, dirty little room lit by a fierce glow from the contents of a burning frying-pan. Cursing mightily, he reached for the pan, remembering only just in time to wrap the scorching-hot handle in a scrap of cloth, before wrenching open the door and throwing the whole thing into the alley, much to the annoyance of a passing cur whose head it missed by bare inches. So occupied was Jackie with his culinary endeavours that he failed to see the two figures who slipped through the doorway behind him and made their way in swift silence up the hotel's main staircase.

'We should be OK, as long as he don't smell the coal-oil in that pan,' Wheeler offered thoughtfully, as he eased the door closed after the girl. Mona looked at him in amazement.

'Ain't you got no nerves at all?' she demanded. Wheeler shrugged indifferently.

'I guess they kinda got lost somewhere back along the way,' he said shortly. 'And, right now, I'm more interested in this.' He held up the wooden writing-case.

Working swiftly, Wheeler placed the battered lamp on the room's solitary table, then positioned the case in the pool of light. With his pocket-knife, he carefully eased back the catch and lifted the lid.

Nothing the case contained seemed to justify Wheeler's caution. There were a few letters, carelessly stuffed back in their envelopes, one or two torn, apparently by their owner's carelessness. Wheeler grunted meaningfully.

'Looks to me like someone else has been here in front of us,' he stated, indicating the half-torn letters. 'Man like Collins ain't that careless with his own stuff.'

Swiftly, he examined the contents of the case. Then he sat back with a frown.

'Nothing!' he snapped, half to himself, 'Unless. . . ' Carefully, he closed the little case, turning it round so

74

that the lid itself was under the light.

The top of the case was plain, except for a small, neatly carved leaf set in the back edge. Carefully, Wheeler pushed the leaf towards the back of the case, but nothing moved. Nor was pushing in any other direction any more successful, until as a last hope, Wheeler put his thumb in the centre of the leaf and pushed down. Sluggishly, the leaf descended and when he could move it no more, Wheeler pushed the leaf forward. There was a satisfying click and the lid was suddenly in two parts.

With the blade of his knife, Wheeler carefully separated the two pieces. Briefly, he examined the top section, carefully keeping his fingers away from the edge.

'Don't touch that,' he ordered shortly, as he placed the section on the floor, 'there's a needle just where a man's finger'd go if he picked it up, and it ain't there for fun.'

The bottom section of the lid contained a single sheet of much-folded, yellowing paper. Wheeler lifted this on the knife blade and, after scanning the contents, he sat back and pushed himself away from the table.

'That's it,' he said simply. 'What Collins was killed for.' He turned away as the girl scanned the paper. The note was brief and to the point.

'At Dead Horse water-hole, follow the trail of the tree at noon, down the crack, to the cave of the Eagle's Claw, and the money is where only a Mouse can go.' She glanced casually at the bottom of the brief note, then stiffened. It was signed 'Levinson'. Mona looked up.

'What's it mean?' she asked despairingly.

Wheeler shrugged. 'Pretty plain that the first thing to do is find the water-hole. Then just take it from there. Get your stuff,' he ordered, turning out the lamp and moving silently to the door. For a moment he listened, then apparently satisfied, he motioned her forward.

'Gotta find you a safe place. Guess Horse-thief'll know somewhere,' he whispered briefly. He led the way out of the door and down the lightless back-stairs.

They reached the rear door of the hotel without incident and Wheeler listened again, this time for longer. Eventually, he drew back and shook his head.

'Sounds OK,' he whispered, 'but we'll go quiet just the same.' Carefully, he eased open the door, barely an inch at a time, but, despite his caution, the hinges gave forth a minute groan. Instantly, Wheeler stopped. For a second he seemed lost in thought then drawing down the girl's head, he whispered:

'Spit on them hinges. Gotta fix 'em so's they don't squeak.'

Obediently, the girl went to work as Wheeler eased the door open, the lubricated hinges now giving off no sound. The opening was barely a foot across when the detective stopped and signed the girl forward.

Obediently, she eased through and stood erect, just as the moon came from behind a cloud and flooded the alley with silvery light. To Wheeler's night-adapted senses, it seemed like glaring daylight and he opened his mouth to caution her as she stepped away from the concealing shadow of the building. But it was too late.

Before the words could leave his mouth, there was the crash of a shot, flame lanced from the shadows and with a little hiccuping sigh, the girl collapsed limply into the dirt of the street.

Wheeler didn't bother to check. He'd heard that sound too many times to hold out much hope of the girl's survival. Instead, he wormed swiftly back through the open door and sent three shots, as fast as he could pull the trigger, into the shadow from which the fatal bullet had come. There was no response but what he did hear was Rolo's voice from Main Street.

'Get down here, you men,' the deputy yelled. 'Girl's bin killed down there and the fella that did it's run into the hotel.' There was an indistinct blur of voices then Rolo's was raised above the din.

'Yeah,' the fat man bellowed, 'I seen who did it! That drifter Wilson. And don't no one bother with a rope. I want the bastard alive!'

CHAPTER NINE

For a long moment, Wheeler hugged the comparative safety of the hotel's rickety back door, mind racing. Rolo had outplayed him, no mistaking that.

Clearly, it was Rolo who'd been waiting in the shadows, gunned down the girl, then immediately slipped away in order to set the hunt after Wheeler.

Probably figured she knew too much, Wheeler thought as he came to a half crouch. Rapidly, he scanned the darkness opposite, then set off at a dead run, angling for the opposite wall and the welcome shadow it offered. Anywhere, came the thought, desperate and unbidden, out of this moonlight.

But his luck seemed suddenly to have turned all bad. He had barely left the door's fragile shelter, when a figure burst from the shadows opposite. Wheeler caught moonlight against the swinging rifle butt barely in time to duck and catch most of the glancing impact on the crown of his Stetson. The blow was hard enough to stun but Wheeler's response, though groggy, was instant. His arm lifted, pushing the man off balance and then his knee hammered in, swift as a rattler's strike. His attacker yelped in agony, twisting away, and Wheeler raced on, shaking his head to clear it. One thing was certain. He had to have somewhere to hide.

Tex Hewitt, known to friends and enemies alike as 'Horse-thief', had just finished his nightly chores. Gratefully, he placed the hay-fork and water-bucket on their respective hooks and moved stiffly towards the door of his little bedroom-cum-parlour, all thoughts centred on a pre-dinner cup of coffee followed by a good meal. He pushed aside the frayed curtain that covered the opening and had taken barely two steps into the room before an ominous double click told him he was not alone.

'Put 'em up!' snarled a muffled voice. Instead of obeying, Hewitt hooked both thumbs into his worn old belt with the silver Lone Star buckle and asked:

'D'you kill 'er, boy?'

There was a brief, menacing silence, then the tension left the room as Wheeler said:

'Nope, that was Rolo. And I'm tellin' you he made a neat job of pulling it off and framing me at the same time. I must be gettin' old and stupid,' Wheeler stated irritably, ' 'cause I never figured that son of a whore was smart enough to open his mouth afore he started eatin'.'

'Uh huh,' Hewitt grunted in sympathy as he lit the lamp and pushed Wheeler towards a vacant chair.

'You et?' the old man demanded and when Wheeler shook his head, Hewitt began slicing bacon into a spluttering pan.

'Confession's best on a full stomach,' he said laconically.

'So where's this letter now?' Hewitt demanded after Wheeler had finished his story.

'I burnt it,' the detective lied, watching the man across the desk intently. But Hewitt's poker-face had had fifty years' practice and barely a muscle twitched as he said unconcernedly:

'So now you're the only one who knows where Levinson's gold is?'

Wheeler nodded then said with a lightness he didn't feel:

'Guess it's up to you to keep me alive, if'n you want a cut.'

Hewitt nodded thoughtfully.

'That may take some doin',' he said bluntly. 'I found out something while you was away. Thunderhead was doped. And I'm figuring Rolo and that slimy horn-toad Blagg was behind it.'

Hewitt's story was briefly told. Some years previously, Waco's Find had held a horse-race. Ponies had come in from all over the territory and the purse had swollen to a massive $10,000.

'Which was won by Fatso Blagg's thoroughbred.' Hewitt explained. 'Only thing was, after the race, that horse was crazy. No one could get near it. Ended up lockin' it in my barn. Next day, though, he was fine, apart from drinkin' 'bout a hundred gallons o' water. I checked around, me and the Marshal, but never found nothin',' he finished.

'What's this got to do with Thunderhead?' Wheeler asked.

'When I cleaned out his stall day after he jumped you, I found this,' Hewitt explained, rummaging in a nearby drawer and finally pulling a strangely shaped bottle into the light.

Wheeler accepted the bottle and gingerly sniffed at the opening. There was nothing except a faint scent of herbs and Wheeler shook his head as he handled the bottle back.

'Don't mean nothing to me,' he admitted, as Hewitt carefully replaced the bottle in its hiding place.

The old man grinned. 'I suppose it shows what a blameless life you've led,' he cackled, 'although it ain't such a common trick as that. What's in the bottle is peyote. Or at least,' he corrected himself as he saw Wheeler's eyes widen, 'it's a special mixture the Apache use on their war ponies, if they're being chased or such like.'

Wheeler studied the old man for a while then asked:

'So you figure Blagg and Rolo killed Collins and've been tryin' to get rid o' me since I got here?'

Hewitt shrugged. 'Looks like that to me,' he offered.

Wheeler nodded. Any number of holes in the old man's argument presented themselves, but the detective held his peace. Hewitt might be pure as the driven snow but if not . . . Wheeler was a great believer in the old proverb about rope and hanging.

'So what do you figure we should do now?' he asked.

'I guess it'd make sense to head off after the money,' Hewitt suggested.

Wheeler nodded and remarked, incidentally, 'Guess it sure musta galled ol' Levi when he was waiting to be hung, knowin' all that money was just sittin' there waiting for him and not a blame thing he could do about it.'

'Levinson weren't hung!' Hewitt spat incautiously, then cursed under his breath. Wheeler looked his surprise and Hewitt explained briefly:

'Shot trying to get away night before they was due to swing. Judge had 'em strung up anyway, he said on account o' so many folks coming so far and him not wantin' them to miss a free show, it bein' election year.'

Wheeler nodded as the wheels churned in his mind.

'How'd they catch 'em alive? I heard that the old man was as mean as a wolverine and the boys was no better.'

Hewitt shrugged with a nonchalance he was far from feeling.

'They was camped, in a little clearing back over yonder, just outside town. Musta caught 'em just before they come in to do the job. They was just waitin' around,' Hewitt explained unwillingly, 'probably for sundown.' Or mebbe for someone, Wheeler thought, eyeing his companion in a new and more suspicious light.

Just at that moment, a fat man was examining a blackened frying-pan, which he had found lying outside the back door of the hotel, where, earlier that night, it had narrowly missed the head of a stray dog. Cautiously, he passed it in front of his nose, recoiling as he recognized the tarry odour of the liquid it contained. For a moment, he paused, weighing the cheap utensil in his hand. Then he dashed it to the floor with an oath and walked rapidly in the direction of the livery stable.

'If that son of a bitch is tryin' to cross me . . .' the man gritted, pausing to pull at the sleeve of his expensive broadcloth, 'I'll . . .' the rest was lost in the surrounding darkness as he increased his pace in the direction of his intended victim.

Wheeler had been long gone as Horse-thief Hewitt made his silent way back to the livery barn, after his nightly visit to the Busted Dollar. Hewitt never gambled and he drank beer only in moderation and spirits never, but he was lawman enough to know that there was no better place to pick up news than a saloon and he desperately needed to know how the hunt for Wheeler was progressing. They'd planned to rendezvous some-where on the trail to the mountains north of town where Hewitt knew Dead Horse water-hole was situated. Wheeler wouldn't be specific about what happened after that and Hewitt was wise enough not to press him.

As far as Hewitt was concerned, the evening had been a success. Disgruntled man-hunters had filled the long bar and there had been many expressions of disgust at the way the hunted man had seemed to vanish into thin air. Finally satisfied that his intended victim was safe, Hewitt had left the bar and was approaching the side-door of the livery stable, when a pair of meaty hands grabbed him by the collar and slammed him back against the sun-dried woodwork.

'Now, you double crossin' ol' bastard, we're gonna have a little talk. . . .' But this wasn't the first time the old livery man had been jumped and even as the words left his attacker's mouth, Hewitt allowed his knees to sag, dragging the man off balance. He twisted, and as the man staggered, trying to steady himself, Hewitt slammed a knee up between his legs, while almost simultaneously driving his forehead into the other's face. Instantly, the hands were jerked from his collar and by the time Hewitt's attacker had recovered, he found himself staring into the bore of the old man's worn Frontier Colt while a cracked, vicious voice was saying:

'Why in hell'er you jumping me?'

'That goddamn Wilson,' the other moaned, massaging the damaged area gingerly, 'he tricked Jackie out o' the hotel and he musta searched Ro . . . Collins's bag. When you wasn't here, I figured mebbe you'd decided you didn't need a partner.'

'And I just sashayed over to the saloon 'cause I felt like a glass o' beer afore I lit out!' Hewitt sneered. First off,' the old man continued, 'I know Wheeler searched Collins stuff 'cause he come and tol' me. And he's done better'n either of us, 'cause he's found the letter.' Briefly, Hewitt described Wheeler's visit and the arrangements the two men had put in place.

'Now all you gotta do is follow along behind and when we find the place and get the money, well, you can stage a little stick-up. Me and Wheeler go back to town cursin' our luck and you and me split the dollars.'

'Sounds OK,' the other admitted cautiously, 'but I'd be happier if that bastard never took the trail back to town.'

Hewitt's Colt lifted meaningly.

'No killing,' he said softly. 'Bodies have a way of turning up. Speakin' o' which, Wheeler found Collins. Cut up worse than a squaw would've done. Know anything about that?'

'Hell, no,' his companion snapped, but the vehemence had a hollow ring and not for the first time,

Hewitt regretted his choice of confederate. But the old man practised his own curious sort of morality and to him a deal was a deal, whoever he contracted it with.

'Follow me out of town tomorrow, 'bout an hour after I leave,' he ordered, turning away. 'I've got some red calico so it'll be easy trailin'.' With his back turned, Hewitt could not see the sneer of virulent hatred which crossed the other man's face.

'The hold-up is a good idea, you old buzzard,' his companion sneered as Hewitt entered the barn and slammed the door, 'but corpses is better and there won't be anyone digging them up this time!'

Small towns are surprisingly difficult to get out of, if you're a fugitive with your face known, but Wheeler was almost at the edge of town before he ran into trouble.

He had slipped round the corner of an old adobe and was making his way cautiously past its rickety corral, when there was a shout and four figures leapt at him out of the darkness.

Wheeler's fist smashed into the face of the first man as he went backwards but the others were clearly experienced and before the detective could move, a rope had pinned his arms. After a brief, vicious skirmish, he found himself tripped and neatly tied. Wheeler's first attacker had recovered enough to stand and he slammed a vicious kick into the bound man's side. Abruptly, one of the others knocked him down.

'What in hell d'you do that fer?' the abused one whined.

'Windy, it was a good idea to stake out this trail out o' town but he's fought us fair, whatever Rolo says he's done, and you ain't gonna abuse him when he's tied and can't defend hisself.' The moon shone briefly on the face of the speaker, who turned out to be Ed Harris, the little storekeeper.

'At least, you ain't while I can pull a trigger,' the little man continued meaningfully, dropping a hand to his holstered Colt.

Wheeler had made something of a study of men in such situations and it was clear to him that this was no bluff. That must have been plain to the one he had knocked down too, because the man rose to his feet with no more than a few grumbles.

'Pick 'im up,' the little storekeeper ordered, 'and we'll go the back way. He may be guilty but he's still entitled to a trial and it'd be best if we keep 'em away from them fools talking "rope".'

'Huh,' grunted one of his companions who had not previously spoken. 'He may be glad of a rope, after Rolo gets through with him, Ed.'

CHAPTER TEN

To Wheeler, in his bound and almost terminally uncomfortable state, the journey to the marshal's office seemed endless but, in reality, not many minutes had elapsed before they reached the back door of the sprawling adobe, where Harris knocked softly.

Abruptly, the door was flung open and the figure of Rolo stood in the doorway.

'Wharinhell d'you want?' he demanded and Wheeler heard one of his captors sneer:

'Killer on the loose and this dumbcluck's hittin' the bottle. Christ!'

Harris must have taken something of the same view because he elbowed the big man unceremoniously aside and snapped:

'Just bring him in here and put him in an empty cell!' As the grinning men complied and Harris snatched the keys from their hook, clearly ready to lock the prisoner in, Rolo stumbled uncertainly forward. He weaved to a halt in front of Harris and whined:

'You may be justice o' the peace, but I'm the law here. It's my job to take in prisoners!'

'You ain't the law! ' Harris snapped. 'Fowler is and a damn poor job he's makin' if he's got to employ the likes o' you.' The little man's lip curled as he finished. 'Whyn't you just go and sleep it off?'

'Goddammit,' Rolo began, 'he's my prisoner. . . .' But that was as far as he got. Harris whipped round to face him, dropping, as he did so, into a relaxed crouch which did Wheeler's heart good. His hand hung easily next to the butt of his Colt as Harris said caustically:

'Now listen, you fat fool. I've lived in this country fifty-some years and I've carried a gun most o' that time, 'cause o' rattlers and other types o' vermin just like you. I know all about *Ley fuego* and that ain't happening here! Likewise, that boy is coming into court tomorrow jist like he is now.' Harris's finger rose and prodded Rolo's greasy vest for emphasis.

'Understand, you blob o' lard?' he continued, 'Just like he is now.' Harris's hand flickered and his Colt was menacing the end of Rolo's nose. 'And if he ain't just like he is now, me and Judge Colt here will be opening a line o' questioning for the defence which you may find extremely painful.' The Colt was back in its holster and Harris slapped the keys into Rolo's filthy vest.

'Lock 'im up,' was the little man's parting shot, 'and don't touch 'im less'n your neck don't suit you the length it is!'

Harris was almost at the doorway when Wheeler called,

'Hey mister.'

The little man turned and his voice was mild as he said, 'Yeah?'

'If you're interested in knowing what really

88

happened to that girl, check for sign behind the hotel. You might want to see which way she was facin' when she was shot,' Wheeler offered.

Harris nodded. 'I might just do that,' he agreed, snapping a last meaningful look at the massive deputy.

Wheeler had been alone long enough for the circulation to return to his hands and feet after the removal of his bonds, when the deputy returned.

But he was a very different figure from the ludicrous picture which had greeted Wheeler's captors. For one thing he was almost sober. And carrying a chair. Rolo placed his burden next to the bars where Wheeler was leaning on the bed, enjoying the single undamaged cheroot he'd managed to salvage from the collection in his pocket. Carefully, the deputy eased into his seat and began to construct a smoke. With the cigarette burning to his satisfaction, he flicked a shred of tobacco from his tongue and said:

'You and me better have a little talk, Wilson, if that's your name.'

'It's as good as any other,' Wheeler said easily, 'and if you want to talk, well . . .' he paused and looked around, 'I ain't goin' anywhere for a while.'

Rolo paused, as though digesting this priceless nugget, then rumbled:

'You was in the hotel tonight and you tricked Jackie away from the front desk somehow, then you went lookin' for somethin' in the back room. What was it?'

Wheeler blew out a lungful of smoke, looked idly at the end of his cigar and said casually:

'Don't know what you're talkin' about, deppity.'

'Goddammit,' Rolo thundered, rising angrily. 'You

found out somethin' about where them dollars are! You better tell me you bastard or. . . .'

'Or nothing!' said a cracked voice followed by an ominous click, and Wheeler could have laughed out loud at the sight of a figure, masked and coated and spurred, standing in the doorway of the office.

'Get the keys, you fat-gutted bastard,' the figure snapped, and as Rolo, white and shaking, moved to obey, the figure stepped to the bars, shoved Wheeler's pistols swiftly through the opening and whispered in Horse-thief Hewitt's cracked tones,

'Cover 'im, boy. And in case you didn't know, we ain't out o' the woods yet, not by a damn sight!'

'Where in hell did you find this crow-bait?' Wheeler demanded disgustedly, as they left the shadow of the jail's veranda and moved towards the hitch rail.

'Beggars can't be choosers.' Hewitt snapped crossly, 'and they'll do fur what we want. Or I should say,' the old man cackled, 'fur what you want!' Suddenly serious, Hewitt pointed and snapped:

'Cut down that alley pronto. Git around behind the saloon 'til you can see the trail outta town. Wait 'til them fellas watchin' it hightail it this way, then ride like hell!'

'Good plan, Horse-thief,' Wheeler sneered, ' 'cept for one little item. Accordin' to what you told me, I'll be goin' exactly the wrong way!'

'Just shet your mouth and listen,' the old man snapped, 'I ain't finished explainin' yet! See the little pinto mare?' he demanded. 'She's in season. Bin bustin' her breeches to get out and find herself a stud.

You take that bay and then peel off about a mile outta town and leave them ponies to it. She'll lead 'em all up into the mountains. Probably won't stop running 'til Christmas.' Hewitt finished, then added, when he saw Wheeler's doubtful look: 'Don't worry. They'll come home when they get hungry and thirsty enough. You better get moving.'

Wheeler nodded and swung into the saddle. As he gathered the reins, he demanded, without looking down:

'Where you gonna be?'

Hewitt laughed softy. 'Aim to get me an alibi,' he admitted. 'I'll be heading fur the mountains sometime tomorrow. Meet up with me like we planned and we'll collect the dollars.'

'So just what do you plan to do about this murdering bastard, Marshal?' Rich Blagg demanded.

News of Rolo's discomfiture had spread quickly with the coming of daylight and a mob of the town's more unsavoury elements had gathered outside the jail even more rapidly. Fowler appeared lost for a reply and Blagg continued contemptuously:

'Since our marshal appears to think it's OK for murdering scum to come into town and butcher our women folk . . .'

'Your womenfolk, Fatso,' a voice called from the crowd. Blagg joined in the muted laugh.

'Well, whoever she belonged to,' the fat man continued, 'I say he shouldn't be allowed to get away with it!'

Fowler waited until the din had subsided before holding up his hands, palms out, and whining:

'Now hold on. O' course, we're goin' after him but it'll be as a properly constituted posse, not a lynch mob.' He almost yelped the last word and without pause, went on: 'Me and Rolo'll go and I reckon we'll only need a tracker and a couple more.' Pausing, Fowler scanned the crowd then snapped:

'What about it, Hewitt, can you track this fella? Usual rates,' he said swiftly as the other opened his mouth.

'Mighty kind o' you, Marshal,' the old man offered, leaning on a battered stick as he limped heavily forward, 'but I done throwed ma knee out agin. Couldn't sit a horse to save my life.'

'Shame about your tracker,' Blagg sneered. 'But I'd like to come, and I'll bring a couple of my boys,' he offered, indicating a hard-faced, gun-hung trio behind him. 'They've had some, eh . . . experience in matters of this sort, you might say,' he added.

'They look right handy,' Rolo offered with an enthusiasm he was far from feeling, 'and I know a real good tracker.'

Fowler sighed, apparently caught in a cleft stick of his own making.

'OK,' he said at last, indecisively. 'Be back here with your horses and gear in a half hour.' He watched as the crowd dispersed, then a hard sneer replaced his habitual good-humoured smile.

'Come one, come all,' he sneered, 'the more witnesses the better!'

Three hours after sundown found Hewitt pushing his favourite pony easily along a plain trail, heading for the mountains.

He had just carefully deposited a piece of red calico

on a convenient bush, when a whipporwill called from the trail ahead. Rapidly, the bird repeated the call twice and Hewitt eased his Colt back into its worn holster. Being careful to keep his hands in sight, he kneed his mount up the trail until suddenly a hard voice said behind him.

'You took your time!'

Hewitt shrugged as Wheeler moved up beside him.

'I'm took sick with a misery in ma leg,' the old man chuckled. 'Where's your pony?'

Wheeler shrugged. 'Camped just off the trail,' he admitted.

'Get him,' Hewitt ordered. 'We ain't doing no movin' by daylight on this job.'

Dawn found the unlikely pair skirting the foot of the mountains where Hewitt eventually found a small hollow a short distance from what passed for the main trail. It wasn't deep enough to keep the wind off and there was no water fit even for the little South-Western mustangs, but it did possess one advantage instantly appreciated by both men.

From its southern edge, their back trail was visible for miles.

With horses cared for and a frugal meal cooked and eaten, they flipped a coin and Wheeler having won, rolled into his blankets, leaving Hewitt the first watch.

'How long you figure that li'l trick with the horses'll hold 'em for?' Wheeler asked sleepily, from the depths of his bed-roll.

'If'n they leave the tracking to Rolo or Fatso,' Hewitt chuckled, 'we'll be in San Francisco afore they figure out what's happened!' Abruptly, he sobered, 'May hold 'em for a day, I reckon, if we're lucky.'

Hewitt couldn't know it but their luck had just run out.

Half a mile down the trail from the point where Wheeler had pulled up the little bay mustang and headed back for the clearing outside of town where he had left Hassan, Pedro got slowly to his feet, carefully dusted the knees of his filthy jeans and spat eloquently into the dust.

'Only four ponies now, *señor*, and none have riders.' he said shortly.

Rolo cursed.

'What you figure he's done?' ge demanded.

Pedro shrugged.

'Is an old trick, *señor*.' He sneered.

'Let the ponies run and then you double back. Work best if they are thirsty and try for water. We jus' look along the trail, find where he leave it and follow him.'

'How long will it take, damn you?' Rolo snapped.

The Mexican's face darkened at the curse, then he shrugged and said:

'Who knows, *señor*? There is a lot of trail and only me to look.'

Muttering savagely, Rolo stamped across to the mounted group halted a little way down the trail. When the deputy had finished his report, one of Blagg's men snapped:

'Does that greaser know what he's doin'?'

'Shut up, Wint,' Blagg ordered without heat, ignoring Fowler. 'You and Kelly and Vittorio go see if you can speed him up. And don't forget. If Wilson gets away, no one gets paid.'

Wint nodded shortly and rode forward, followed by his two companions.

'Funny 'bout that greaser,' Blagg went on. 'I'm sure I recognize 'im.'

Rolo said nothing but the sweat began to break out of his pores. This little game was starting to get dangerous.

It took Pedro less than an hour to locate the place where Wheeler had turned off, and he led the way along the trail the detective had left, almost at a trot.

For hours the little Mexican rode tirelessly, until, suddenly, the men following saw him pull up and swing down from the saddle. Briefly, he examined something on the side of the trail, then he beckoned Rolo forward. As the big man rode up, Pedro held out his hand. Stretched across the palm was a piece of red calico. Rolo cursed and clenched his fist.

'Goddamitt,' he swore, 'that son of a bitch weren't wearing nothin' like that! We bin followin' the wrong man!' The Mexican raised his eyes heavenwards at yet more evidence of his gringo partner's stupidity.

'No, *amigo*,' he explained patiently, 'this was tied to the bush.'

Rolo looked blank, and the Mexican continued:

'Looks to me like someone is leavin' a trail. Mebbe there will be more.'

Some three hours later, as the sun was beginning its afternoon dip towards the horizon, Wheeler found himself roughly shaken awake.

'Get up,' Hewitt snapped, 'we got company!'

CHAPTER ELEVEN

Blearily rubbing sleep from his eyes, Wheeler followed Hewitt across the camp-ground and flopped down next to him. Carefully removing his battered Stetson, the detective edged forward until his eyes were just above the rim of the little basin.

'There. See 'em?' the old man demanded. Clear against the crystal mountain-light, the tiny figures represented a stark contrast. Mouthing silently, Wheeler counted, then counted again.

'I make it seven,' he said eventually. 'Know any of them?'

'No,' Hewitt admitted, stifling his rage. Goddamn that fat fool, the old man thought, how can we lose seven of them? Aloud, he snapped:

'We gotta blind our trail.'

'Got any ideas?' Wheeler asked evenly.

His companion nodded.

'Mebbe I can remember a li'l trick or three,' the old man offered. 'Saddle them ponies, while I get some stuff. And rip up one o' them blankets and muffle their hoofs with it.'

Some time later, as the sun slipped below the horizon, Wheeler and Hewitt lay on a slab of rock overlooking their night camp, watching with satisfaction as Pedro led his party down on the trail that Hewitt had made with a couple of spare horseshoes that he had brought for just that purpose. Hewitt grunted as the two men pushed away from the edge and went to collect their horses, but, plainly, the grunt held little of satisfaction.

'What?' Wheeler asked.

'I know that greaser bastard,' his companion admitted. 'He was raised by the Kiowas and he's gonna be tricky to fool. Keep them blankets on them ponies' hoofs while they last. We can't overlook no bets.' Hewitt swung into his saddle, adding nervously, 'we best make tracks.'

'No,' Wheeler said shortly. 'I ain't goin' treasure hunting through these mountains with a posse nor nothin' else on my tail.' He paused, clearly thinking, before demanding: 'You say this greaser is pretty good?'

Hewitt nodded.

Wheeler said: 'Then this is what we do do. . . .' When he had finished, Hewitt gave him a look of deep disgust and snapped:

'Suppose your hunches don't pan out?'

Wheeler shrugged. 'Then you'll have to think of somethin'.'

Down below, riding the trail out of the little hollow, Rolo grunted with porcine satisfaction.

'That ol' bastard must be slipping. Pedro,' he told his companion. 'Even I could foller this trail.'

'Oh this is not their trail, *señor*,' said the little man,

'Señor Hewitt make this with two old horseshoes.' Before Rolo could express his astonishment, his companion went on:

'They are watching to see where we go. I make them think they fool us. In the dark, we go back and camp in their place. They will think we are far behind. Ride slow, mebbe stop. Tomorrow we find their trail and catch them. Then . . .' the hand signal, even in the dark, was graphic and Rolo grinned his admiration.

'Pedro,' he offered, 'you sure got a head. Them dollars is as good as ours.'

The sun had been gone for many hours and the cold of the high country night was beginning to bite. Which didn't help the temper of the man guarding the posse's camp.

'Goddamn pair o' fat bastards!' Wint, the luckless individual in question, swore, 'I sure hate a son of a bitch who won't do his share!' Both Fowler and Blagg had made it quite clear that they would not be standing a turn on watch, which together with the cold and cigaretteless dark accounted for Wint's bad temper.

Suddenly, the man stiffened. Somewhere, through the crystal stillness, a noise had drifted. Just once, but it had seemed to come from the direction of the horses.

Following usual cowboy practice, the horses were all tied to a single line that had been stretched between two convenient trees. Wint breathed a sigh of relief as he approached and saw that all seemed well with the herd.

'Phew,' Wint said to no one in particular, resting his Winchester carefully against a nearby tree and reaching for his tobacco and papers, 'must be getting old and nerv . . .' He never finished because at that precise moment the ivory butt of a Smith & Wesson revolver slammed into the side of his head.

For a moment, his assailant bent, roughly checking the body, then he rose and Cord Wheeler's voice called softly:

'All right, Hoss-thief, turn 'em loose.'

Dawn found the posse and, in particular Marshal Fowler, in a less than sanguine frame of mind.

'So who the hell was it, Wint?' the fat man snapped. The gunman shook his head and groaned at the result of his experiment. Fowler threw up his hands in frustration.

'What in hell d'we do now?' he demanded of no one in particular. 'And where in hell is that greaser?' At that moment, Pedro appeared, with the little dun mustang that he habitually rode following obediently behind him. Eyeing the almost apoplectic Fowler, he said softly,

'Maybe there is somethin' I can do for the *señor*?' Before anyone could speak, he went on, looking at Rich Bragg sitting corpulent and uncomfortable on a discarded saddle: 'For, say, twenty Yankee dollars a pony?'

'You was right, Horse-thief,' Cord Wheeler admitted, as he reached the top of a turn in the vague trail they were following and eased Hassan to a halt, 'that greaser is sure a tricky li'l bastard. Where you figure he had that pony?'

Hewitt spat eloquently and said:

'Next to his blanket, with double hobbles, back and front. He's been chased before. I'm admittin' it would have been a good plan if'n it had worked,' Hewitt continued, 'but he ain't gonna be long catchin' up them ponies. You got any other bright ideas?'

Wheeler shrugged. 'Mebbe,' he admitted, 'but you know the country and I'm sure admitting it'd be better if we could lose 'em.'

'I reckon our best play is Avalanche Canyon,' Hewitt offered after a moment's thought. 'It ain't on the way to where we're goin' but there's rock and good places for hiding tracks. And we can cut back through a little pass I know to the water-hole without losin' too much time. Also,' he finished, 'it's about the last thing that tricky greaser'll expect.'

Wheeler nodded. 'Lead on, Macduff,' he said facetiously. He might not have remembered it, but there's some folks'll tell you quoting *Macbeth* can be awful unlucky.

Dusk was a bare hour away when Hewitt drew rein and said softly:

'Well, here she be.'

Wheeler nodded, briefly scanning the dark and inhospitable cut that Hewitt indicated, before turning and making a careful study of their back trail. Apparently satisfied, he turned again and said:

'No sign behind us. Guess we must have lost 'em.'

Hewitt nodded, already kneeing his pony forward. As they reached the rock-littered entrance to the canyon, the old man whispered:

'This ain't called Avalanche Canyon for nothing. Don't make no more noise than you can help and if'n you feel like pullin' a gun, better use it to shoot yourself. You'll find it'll be quicker that way,' he finished callously.

100

There was obviously little light in the canyon at the best of times and with dusk approaching, it seemed as if night had already fallen inside. Hewitt allowed his mount to proceed at little more than a walk and Wheeler let Hassan amble after him, reins slack so that the clever little Arab could pick his own way. For what seemed like an eternity they scrabbled across the boulder-and-scree-strewn floor until eventually, rounding a jutting angle of rock, Wheeler saw, a little way ahead, a patch of lighter sky between two rock faces. Hewitt must have seen it too, because he turned.

'Entrance ahead,' he whispered. 'Thank Gawd, we're nearly thr . . .' That was as far as he got. Suddenly, from a crevice near his pony's feet there came a vicious whirr. Startled by the rattler's warning, Hewitt's mount shied savagely and the old man gave a cry of surprise as he was thrown from the saddle and deposited inches from the snake, lying coiled and ready to strike. Startled in its turn, the rattler reared back, before lunging forward, mouth wide, inches-long fangs ready to sink into the flesh of Hewitt's face or neck. Instinctively, Hewitt jerked back, as the sound of a shot echoed in his ear and the snake's head neatly disintegrated into a wreck of bone and gristle.

Shakily, the old man passed a hand across his face as he got to his feet and said,

'Th-th-thanks, Cord, I sure thought I was a goner. . . .'

A low rumble interrupted him, causing both men to look up. High on the wall of the canyon, several large rocks had dislodged themselves and came skittering down the rock face. The rumble came again, deeper

101

this time, more ominous as, without any warning, a six-foot slab of rock disengaged itself from the overhang and began to slide towards the trail, towards the exact spot where the two men were standing.

'Christ,' Hewitt screamed. 'Avalanche! Get out while you can!' Swift as thought, Wheeler jerked out his revolver and fired twice across the rumps of the pack-horse and Hewitt's recalcitrant mount. With a scream of terror, the canny little pinto took off for the exit, followed by the other animal, as, with barely a loss of movement, Wheeler shoved the weapon into his belt and wheeled the nervous Hassan towards the light patch at the end of the canyon. More rock had begun to detach itself from the surrounding walls as Wheeler kneed Hassan to full gallop and headed towards his companion.

'Grab on!' was all Wheeler managed to gasp, and it was barely enough. Hewitt had only time to lift his arms before Wheeler had grabbed the front of his shirt, hauling his burden across the horn of the saddle and then urging Hassan on towards the gap in the rock. On hammered the little Arab's rock-hard hoofs, never faltering. To Wheeler, the trail to safety seemed endless, but in reality, bare seconds had passed before Hassan emerged into the light, as an echoing crash signalled that, at least for the moment, Avalanche Canyon was no longer open for business.

Unceremoniously, Wheeler dumped Hewitt on to his feet. As Wheeler swung down and began a swift examination of his pony, Hewitt sank to a nearby rock and said in a quavering voice,

'I-I-I want to thank you, boy. But for you I'd be

lookin' at one of them rocks from the wrong side.'

Wheeler nodded. 'I'll catch up them ponies. Then we gotta move,' he answered, swinging into the saddle.

'Hold hard thar!' Hewitt objected. 'I ain't exactly feelin' like doin' a lot of movin' tonight. I figured we could camp here, push on in the mornin'.'

'What you usin' for brains, Horse-thief?' Wheeler gibed and before the older man could reply, he went on: 'You told me yourself that the greaser knows this country near good as you. Even if he didn't hear the shot, the noise from that rock fall'll have carried for miles. Now, I don't know,' Wheeler continued sarcastically, 'but I'm guessin' there ain't too many places where a thing like that is liable to happen. And if you was huntin' a man and heard . . .'

'I'd high tail here, straight and as quick as I could ride,' the old man snapped an interruption. 'Well,' he demanded, 'what are you waiting fur? Catch up them ponies!'

But Hassan and Wheeler were already gone.

CHAPTER TWELVE

'Waal, there she be,' Horse-thief Hewitt informed Wheeler as they drew rein on a rocky bluff overlooking their destination. 'Ain't much, is it?' the old man demanded when his companion offered no comment.

Wheeler grunted an affirmative. There didn't seem much more to be said.

Dead Horse water-hole consisted of a tiny sump filled to the brim with muddy water, set in a mile-wide basin whose walls seemed wholly made up of scree and blasted rock. Rock walls towered far above the pair as they rode down from the shallow bluff and approached the stagnant water. Yards from the water Hewitt raised a hand. For a moment he studied the ground.

'Fresh tracks,' he grunted.

'Anyone we know?' Wheeler asked brusquely.

The old man shook his head. 'Unshod ponies,' Hewitt stated dismissively. 'Just a coupla braves huntin'. So what now?' he demanded.

Wheeler shrugged. 'We wait,' he said shortly. 'Unless your friends turn up and get ideas.'

With the horses taken care of and Hewitt snoozing in

the shade, Wheeler set about locating the markers described in Levinson's letter.

The first presented little difficulty. Some two hundred yards from the water-hole he found a stunted burr-oak, It had seeded in a sandy crevice and survived somehow until the heat of an unusually vicious summer had dried its heart, leaving nothing but a pathetic stick to serve as a marker for the outlaw hoard. Gently, Wheeler touched the narrow trunk and a faded piece of bark dropped into his hand.

'You ain't gonna tell me much, looks like, old fella,' he murmured. 'Must be nigh on noon now.'

Almost as he spoke, the sun stood clear of the high range that fringed the bowl and blazed through a single gap formed by the angle of two peaks. The blinding light flashed down on the little tree and a giant shadow seemed to leap away, running like smoke towards the opposite wall of rock. Carefully, Wheeler noted the fall of the dark line as he walked slowly towards the rock wall. Then, as suddenly as it had come, the light blinked out and Wheeler was left standing in the shadow of the rock face. Slowly, the man from El Paso raised a hand to scratch under the band of his hat. As his hand fell he began unconsciously to whistle a tune. Hewitt, half-way between sleep and waking, heard and muttered stupidly:

'Who in hell'd be whistling *Shenandoah* in a place like this?'

The old man's siesta was short-lived.

'Need your help, Horse-thief,' Wheeler admitted as he hunkered down next to his companion.

Hewitt nodded. 'You better tell me what them instructions said,' he advised.

*

'Trail of a Tree?' Hewitt asked disbelievingly. 'And you figure you've found the trail?'

'Sure,' Wheeler agreed. 'Only it leads exactly nowhere.'

Standing before the seemingly impenetrable wall of rock, at first Hewitt was inclined to agree. Then his experienced old eyes began to trace the line of boulders before him. He snapped his fingers.

'Get the pick, boy,' he ordered. 'That rock-fall is plumb recent.'

Wheeler nodded. 'I saw that too,' he offered, 'and if'n you climb up a little way you can see where the fella knocked a lot of the loose stuff down. Pretty easy done, too,' he observed. 'Ain't what you might call hard rock. We better go easy if we don't want the whole mountain down on us.'

Several hours' hard digging cleared most of the rubble, to reveal an enormous slab of stone, the height of a man, apparently lying immovable against the cliff. It appeared almost upright and Hewitt scratched his frowzy head at the sight of it.

'What now?' he demanded.

'Guess we gotta move it,' his companion stated.

Wheeler made a careful examination of the stone. Then he stood back and shrugged.

'Don't seem like there's nothing else for it. Give me a hand here, Horse-thief,' he ordered, picking up a shovel and inserting it between the stone and the rock face. The shovel slid in easily and as Wheeler gave an experimental yank, he found himself thrown backwards on to the rock floor, while the stone swung smoothly open, as though on hinges, to reveal a narrow tunnel, perhaps half the height of a man, going slightly uphill into the darkness.

Hewitt gave a whoop of joy and made to start up the tunnel, only to be halted by his companion's voice.

'Wait up, old man,' the detective ordered. 'This may be a longer job than we figured.' He glanced up at the sky. 'Be dark in an hour. Let's find a better place than this to leave those ponies. Money's been there this long, it'll wait a while longer. See if you can close that stone and hide the hole while I pack the stuff.'

Up on the rimrock, Rich Blagg passed a pair of expensive binoculars to the fat, sweating man beside him.

'Looks like they found it,' he stated, with an air of profound satisfaction.

'Yeah,' Rolo offered stupidly, before asking: 'So what do we do now, boss?'

Blagg turned sideways with a sneer.

'We wait, stupid,' he snarled. 'Then, when they've done all the work, we sneak in and collect the dollars!'

Rolo looked dubious. 'I dunno,' he offered. 'Hewitt's a tricky old bastard and Wilson don't seem exactly green. I think . . .'

'You ain't paid to think,' Blagg snapped savagely, 'You're bein' paid to do a job, so shut your mouth and do what you're told.'

'Paid! Goddammit,' Rolo bridled, 'You said . . .'

'Paid.' Blagg nodded. 'Any objections?' he asked silk-ily, hand shoving into a convenient pocket.

'No,' Rolo answered nervously, gulping back his

rage. 'No, wages is all right with me, boss.'

Blagg nodded in satisfaction and turned back to his binoculars, missing as he did so the venemous look of satisfaction the deputy threw in his direction.

That night, seated around the low-burning campfire, Rolo opened his campaign.

'Sure good to know we're gettin' so well paid for this job,' he began clumsily.

Wint looked up and shrugged. 'Seems to me Fatso never paid any more for anythin' than he'd got to. We're barely makin' eatin' money.'

Rolo feigned a look of surprise.

'That so?' he offered, appearing to think. 'That's funny, 'cause Fatso,' he jerked his head to where Blagg and Fowler were seated around a separate fire of their own, 'He figures to make hisself quite a stake out of this li'l business.'

'How,' demanded Jug Kelly, the second of Blagg's men.

'Oh,' Rolo murmured artlessly, 'he aims to find Levinson's dollars!'

Wint, Kelly and the third man, Vittorio, exchanged meaningful glances before Wint drew his Colt and said, balancing the weapon easily in his hand:

'I think you better tell us all about it, deppity. And don't leave nothin' out or. . . .'

Over by the second fire, Blagg said nervously:

'What about Rolo and the old man?'

Fowler shrugged and shook his head.

'Don't see it as a problem, Rich,' he offered easily. 'After all, people dissolve partnerships all the time, don't they.'

108

*

Dawn saw Wheeler and Hewitt back at the rock face.

'Sure wish we didn't have to walk,' Hewitt grumbled.

'Same here,' Wheeler agreed, 'but we may need those ponies in good shape afore this is over, which they won't be if we leave 'em standin' out in the sun with no food nor water. Anyways, walkin' won't hurt you and I'm figurin' we should locate them dollars in a day or two.'

They had discovered a patch of good grazing in a small stand of pines early the previous evening, not far from the basin. A little stream ran through the trees and after spending the night there, Wheeler and Hewitt had hobbled and picketed the ponies on the best of the grass, hidden the riding- and camp-gear under a convenient boulder and walked back to Dead Horse water-hole.

'At least we ain't gotta lug nothing but our rifles,' Wheeler offered.

'And I'm sure hopin' we ain't gonna be needin' them afore this is over,' Hewitt grumbled, slipping his fingers under the rim of the stone and heaving it aside with a jerk. Wheeler gave the narrow sloping tunnel a brief inspection.

'After you, Ranger,' he offered, stepping back.

At first, the way was awkward and narrow, made even more difficult by the rocks liberally scattered over the floor, but soon the tunnel widened and increased in height, until Hewitt suddenly stepped out on to a wide rocky ledge, which wound down towards a low-sided ravine. Wheeler was only a few paces behind his companion and having surveyed the prospect, Hewitt led the way down the gently sloping trail.

Suddenly, Wheeler pulled him to a halt. Stuck in a narrow crevice in the rock, high above the trail the detective had spotted a flash of white. It was a collection of bones and as Wheeler examined it, he could just make out the white frosting of talons at the tip and then, beyond it, a narrow strip of darkness, extending back out of sight. Wheeler nodded, half to himself.

'Cave of the Eagle's Claw, right enough,' he mumbled. 'This is the place, Horse-thief,' he stated, more clearly. 'We may have some climbing to do.'

Between the trail they were standing on and the half-seen entrance, was a slope which seemed to consist mainly of rubble and small boulders. The surface was treacherous and time and again Wheeler lost his footing and slipped back. Luckily, the trail was slightly wider at this point, but Wheeler had more than once been glad of the safety-rope secured round his waist.

At last his scrabbling fingers hooked around the jutting lip of a rock slab and, muscles cracking with effort, he managed to heave himself level with the bones and the black shadow he had seen from the trail.

What had been visible from the trail was in fact the top of a good-sized cave, its entrance at the bottom of a little sloping basin which concealed it from anyone looking up from below.

Thankfully, Wheeler heaved himself over the rim and into the hollow. Far a moment, he heaved air into lungs pushed to the limit by the climb then he turned and waved to Hewitt.

'So what d'you figure this business about a mouse

means?' Hewitt demanded as they stood surveying the interior of the cave, after Wheeler had explained about the last part of the riddle.

'I dunno.' Wheeler shrugged. 'Mice live in holes was about all I could come up with. Or cheese, mebbe,' he added vaguely, looking around the gloomy cavern only faintly lit by the early morning sunlight.

'Mouse, mouse,' Hewitt ruminated. 'There was a Mouse Murphy, rode with Levinson for years,' he began reluctantly. 'Goddam hydrophoby little killer he was too. Some kinda midget or dwarf . . .' his words trailed off as Wheeler snapped:

'Bet your life that's it! Must be a hole in the rock somewheres too small for a man to get down, so you need a Mouse, a Mouse Murphy. Levinson sure must have had a funny sense o' humour,' he finished.

'Son,' Hewitt returned harshly, 'you just don't know the half of it! Let's try over here,' he continued, leading the way towards the back of the cave.

There turned out to be only one hole large enough even after Hewitt and Wheeler had gone over every inch of the walls. Hewitt lit a tiny fire of chips and by the light of a pine-knot, gleaned from the night-camp, Wheeler examined the crevice.

At last he gave a grunt of satisfaction and stood up, massaging his back.

'It's there,' Wheeler stated flatly. 'Old carpet-bag, big one, roped shut. Bad news is, I can't reach it, can't even get close.'

Briefly, Hewitt inspected their find, then stepped back, saying: 'Can we get a rope on it?'

Wheeler shrugged. 'Too cramped. I couldn't throw

111

that far. You'd need arms like tree-trunks. Tree-trunks . . .' he repeated softly, 'that may be the answer. Stay here, Horse-thief,' Wheeler ordered abruptly. 'I just got to fetch somethin'. Break out your lariat while I'm gone and grease the hondo. Make sure it slips real easy.'

Back at the sump, Wheeler wasted no time in going to work. Grasping the top of the little oak which had served as Levinson's finger, he twisted gently until the trunk was loose enough to pull out. As he turned back towards the tunnel with the fragile limb in his hand, up on the rimrock Fowler pocketed his binoculars and began to crawl away. Blagg, who had been lying next to him, turned.

'Where in hell are you goin',' he snapped.

Fowler's big face lit up in a good-humoured smile.

'Why, I'm gonna collect our money,' he answered jovially.

'What makes you think they've found it?' Blagg demanded.

'You figure he wants that chunk o' wood for a walkin'-cane, mebbe?' Fowler sneered. 'Get that scum that works for you movin'. We got work to do.'

CHAPTER THIRTEEN

Back at the cave, Hewitt had been busy in Wheeler's absence.

'Rope's all ready,' the old man assured his companion, taking the length of burr-oak from him as Wheeler swung over the rim.

Curiously, the old man turned the stick over in his gnarled hands then he shrugged and followed Wheeler into the cave, leaving the rope they had used to climb up dangling over the rim.

Wheeler's preparations were soon made.

'Saw this trick once in one o' them rodeo shows,' the detective said as he finished tying Hewitt's rope to the stick with a last piece of twine. A large bight of line and the loop itself now extended past the tip, while the rest of the rope was tightly secured to the stick at intervals. Experimentally, Wheeler shook the contraption, giving vent to a grunt of satisfaction when his knots held.

'Works like this,' Wheeler explained. 'I push the pole as far up that hole as I can. Then I flip the loop over the bag, draw it tight and we haul in the money. What d'you think?'

'Sure,' Hewitt answered sarcastically 'Should only take about a year!'

It didn't take a year but the bag dragged and stuck fast and the rope slipped and the twine broke and so, finally, did the fragile burr-oak. Wheeler was red-faced and nearly hysterical with rage by the time he had managed to drag the bag within hand's reach. So intent were both on the problem presented by the bag that neither paid any attention to the small sounds which drifted in from outside.

'Goddamit, Horse-thief,' Wheeler snapped as he drew the bag from the hole and subsided on to the ground, feeling the rage slip away as fatigue enveloped him. 'I sure hope the goddam bag is worth it!'

The old man nodded. 'So do I, b . . .' he began.

But that was as far as he got. From the shadows which the slanting rays of the noon sun threw into the cave mouth, a figure emerged, with a pistol cocked and ready in his fist.

'Sure nice of you boys to do all the hard part for us,' Wint said, stepping carefully away from the entrance. Without taking eyes or gun off the two men before him, he called over his shoulder: 'Vittorio, get in here, help me with these two. Jug, get them goddam fat green-horns up here. Stand up, you,' he snapped finally, thrusting the barrel of his pistol at Wheeler.

'Well,' Rich Blagg sneered as he waddled clumsily into the cave, carefully rubbing his soft hands where the hard manila had burnt them, 'lookee what we got here, Guess you went a bit too far with this job, Mr Private Detective, didn't you?'

'That's far enough,' Wint snapped as the fat man

114

made to advance on the prisoners. 'We'll just take their guns afore they git any ideas.'

Blagg shook his head as Fowler advanced into the cave and halted a little distance behind him.

'Leave 'em their guns,' the fat saloon keeper ordered, 'and you, greaser,' he snapped,' get on with settin' that dynamite.'

Vittorio made no move to obey and a slow, evil smile spread across his face as he raised his pistol.

'I think, *señor*,' he said, 'ther' has been a so ver' li'l change of plan.'

'Wint!' Blagg roared, 'tell that goddam half-breed to get on with it.' When the one addressed made no move, Blagg screamed, 'Wint, I'm orderin' you.'

Nodding slowly, Wint stepped across the space that separated him from his rotund employer, until he was in easy reach of him. Abruptly, he slashed the barrel of his Colt across Blagg's mouth, knocking him to the floor in the direction of the cave mouth.

'You talk too much,' Wint said softly. 'Like ol' Vitt says, there's been a change of plan. Where d'you put that charge?'

'Just outside the cave, in the wall,' lisped the Mexican. 'The rock face, she is rotten. One little charge, poof, she all come down.'

Wint nodded.

'Good.' Rolo chimed in. 'Now, let's get the dollars and get outta here.'

Wint nodded again.

'We are,' he assured the deputy, 'but you ain't. Get over there with your boss and his fat friend.' Anything else he might have been going to say was lost as Hewitt stormed:

'Goddam it, you fat bastard. You was set to double-cross me and blow this cave in.' Beside himself with rage, Hewitt's hand flashed Colt-ward. But he was too slow. Wint's pistol cracked once and the old man was thrown backwards to smash in to the rock wall and subside into the dirt piled there. Involuntarily, Wheeler stooped, only halted by the sound of Wint cocking his pistol. The dry click echoed through the cave, making Wint's voice loud in the ensuing stillness.

'Now, we'll take the money, mister.'

Wheeler darted one considering glance at Hewitt's body as he straightened. Slowly, he lifted his face until he was looking into Wint's eyes, before putting his head on one side and saying mildly:

'No, I don't think that's a very good idea. I think the marshal should have it!'

As the last word left his lips, Wheeler heaved the bag away, into the centre of the cave. For a split second, Wint's eyes followed it and in that stolen moment in time, Wheeler acted. In one unbelievably swift move-ment, his hand flashed to the butt of the Smith & Wesson. As Wint's eyes flicked back towards him and the killer began to raise his Colt, the muzzle of Wheeler's pistol cleared the edge of his coat and belched flame.

Caught in the chest, Wint was slammed backwards, even as Wheeler dived for cover and a bullet from Jug Kelly's gun cut the air where the man from El Paso had stood a bare split second before. His anxiety to finish Wheeler proved Kelly's undoing, however. He was erect, staring into the gloom at the back of the cave, as Wheeler snapped a second shot and Kelly, caught in the

116

centre of the forehead, spun round, casting away his weapon and slumping to the floor.

Snug behind the inadequate cover of crumbling boulder, Wheeler considered his options. The cave appeared deserted now, even the rope-secured carpet-bag had vanished and more worryingly, there were very significant sounds coming from the entrance. Wheeler spat.

Where in hell was that goddam greaser?

Almost instantly, his question was answered, as Vittorio, panicked by the sounds from outside, rose from his cover and sprinted with desperate speed towards the cave mouth, emptying his weapon wildly into the threatening shadows as he ran. Wheeler acted with characteristic ruthlessness.

Swiftly, he propped his right elbow, sighted, exhaled half a breath and squeezed the trigger. Hit in the chest, Vittorio slumped like a gut-shot rabbit, dying even as he fell. But Wheeler wasn't waiting. The body had barely hit the ground before he was sprinting across the cave floor, slamming into the sunlight just as Rolo disappeared over the rim of the little basin, giving vent to a sneering laugh as he dropped.

Without conscious thought, Wheeler's pistol leapt up, belching flame and Rolo's laugh turned to a yelp of fear as the bullet snatched his filthy hat and sent it spinning into the depths beneath.

Mad with hatred, Wheeler took one step towards the rim of the little bowl, only to come to a sudden halt as an unfamiliar sound knocked on the door of his subconscious. It was a faint hissing and for a moment, he stood wondering until the dead greaser's words came back to him in a frightening rush.

One little charge, poof. . . !

Desperately, Wheeler threw himself back into the cave mouth. He managed four steps into the welcoming darkness, before there was a vicious crump and dust and rocks cascaded into the entrance. Caught by the sidelong thrust of the explosion, Wheeler was thrown forward. His head slammed against the rock wall and he knew no more.

'For Jesus Christ's sake,' Rolo screamed as he slid the last few feet to the trail below the cave, 'that bastard can shoot like hell!' But he was talking to himself. Fowler, followed by a desperately puffing Rich Blagg was disappearing up the trail, the battered carpet-bag clutched in one meaty hand. For a moment, Rolo glared after them, before realization struck and he took to his heels, desperately striving to put enough distance between him and the cave before the mountain crashed down on him.

There were still yards between him and the safety of the tunnel when the charge exploded. Rolo didn't bother to look back, or he would have seen the entire side of the mountain seem to poise itself for a long, breath-drawing instant before hurtling downwards, burying the trail and the cave under hundreds of tons of rotten stone. Using almost the last strength left in his gross body, Rolo dragged himself to safety as a piece of rock the size of a small pony crashed on to the trail behind him, effectively sealing the tunnel mouth for ever.

With lungs on fire and every breath a torment, for a time the fat deputy concerned himself only with respiring. As vision returned, however, he became aware that he was alone in the tunnel.

He struggled to his feet. If Fowler and Blagg reached the horses first, he was well aware of how long they were likely to delay their return journey. Even the presence of Pedro failed to reassure him.

'That son of a bitch ain't gonna let one greaser get in his way, I reckon, not now he's got the loot,' Rolo gasped to himself as he stumbled down the tunnel and in to the sunlight which flooded the little basin.

'Where in Christ's name has that dirty little bastard got to?' Fowler snarled to no one in particular.

'Mebbe he's sleepin'?' Blagg offered diffidently. For a moment, Fowler studied his companion and Blagg repressed a shudder. So might a farmer have examined a new and loathsome pest before he squashed it. Then Fowler smiled expansively.

'No,' he said affably, 'he ain't asleep. He's here. Pedro, *amigo*,' he called, raising his voice. 'Where are the ponies?'

Slowly, the Mexican raised a hand and pushed back his battered sombrero, his face lighting up with a vicious smile.

'They are lost, for the moment, *señor*,' he began, spreading his hands, 'but they can be found again, so verra quickly,' he paused and lisped, 'for, say, half what is in the bag?'

'Half!' Fowler let out a choking laugh. '*Half*! Damned if that ain't right funny. Now, Pedro,' he continued, all humour leaving the big face, 'you get them ponies and you get 'em now, son!'

'Half seems only fair, Señor . . .' Pedro began, stepping forward, but Fowler's arm instantly straightened, there was the snap of a small-calibre pistol and Pedro was clawing at a patch of blood spreading rapidly from the centre of his chest. Suddenly, all strength seemed to leave him and he slumped to his knees and on to his face.

Callously, Fowler shoved a boot under the body and flipped the Mexican on to his back. The eyes, open and sightless, told their own story and the marshal looked across at his companion as he replaced the spent cartridge in his derringer.

'We better find them ponies,' he said softly. Blagg's nod of agreement was frantic with sincerity. His craven heart quailed at what it had just seen and he turned away quickly, anxious to be anywhere but under that cold, speculative stare.

Hidden behind a pine-tree on the lip of the slope which led down to their makeshift camp, Rolo was coming slowly to a similar decision. The marshal was a very unsafe individual to be around at that moment. Even if they found the horses, Rolo could see clearly that Fowler was unlikely to welcome any further claim on the contents of the bag. But what choice was there? Rolo thought desperately. There was plainly no way back to town on foot, even with food and water. Horses, that was the key, horses.

He snapped his fingers, a slow smile spreading across his soiled and repellent features. Wheeler and the old man had horses! And they wouldn't be far away.

Slowly, Rolo edged back to the lip of the campground, until, sure he was invisible any one watching below, he headed back towards the water-hole. After all, he sneered to himself, no one else'd have any use for them ponies. Not now.

CHAPTER FOURTEEN

The groaning beat through the hammering inside Wheeler's skull and dragged him back to consciousness. That and the feeling that he could use a drink of water. About a gallon to start with and then perhaps a couple more for chasers. And with that thought, consciousness returned with a snap.

Not that it appeared to have done much good. Even with his eyes open, the darkness was total and for a moment, Wheeler panicked, wondering if the blow to his head had sent him blind. Gradually, however, he was able to make out features of the cave and returning memory reassured him that the lack of light was to be expected. But not the groaning. As his head cleared, he became more aware of it. Someone was in pain and that someone wasn't too far away.

Slow and silent, Wheeler searched the adjacent floor until he was rewarded by encountering the cold, hard familiarity of the Smith & Wesson. Carefully, he checked the action and the loads, then, soundless as a cat, he crept towards the injured man.

Suddenly, his thrusting hand encountered some-thing warm.

Instantly alert, he jerked his gun towards it as a weak, cracked voice whispered:

'Be that you, boy?' Slipping away the pistol, Wheeler shuffled round next to the injured man.

'Yeah, it's me, Hoss-thief,' he said gently. 'Thought they'd killed you sure.'

'Oh, he done fur me, the sonovabitch,' Hewitt slurred. 'And my so called partner . . .'

'Yeah, he didn't let no grass grow, did he?' Wheeler finished for him.

In the darkness, the detective felt his arm grasped.

'So you guessed, did you, boy? When?' the old man demanded.

'Well, I knew you wasn't what you said from almost the first time I spoke to you.' To save the old man's strength, Wheeler went on quickly: 'When you showed me that Ranger badge, I knew you'd never been a peace officer. You ain't allowed to keep the badge if you ain't in the job. You got to turn it in, so I knew the badge couldn't have bin yourn, and likewise it was a good bet you'd never even worked for the law. As for that other fella, well, he's tricky and pretty smart, but he made a slip early on that set me thinking about him. Never figured you for partners 'til just now, though. He murdered Collins, didn't he?'

Hewitt grunted an affirmative. 'I'm pretty sure it was him,' the old man gasped painfully, 'but I want you to know I never knew nothin' about torturin' that fella 'til you told me. And I ain't tellin' you his name neither.'

'Never figured it for your kinda play,' Wheeler reassured him, 'and I never thought you'd rat on a partner, but how did it all start?'

' 'Bout seven, eight year ago, I was a bounty killer,' Hewitt began bluntly. 'Levinson and his boys had been runnin' wild all over the state since the War, near twenty year, and no one could get a sniff o' them or their hide-out. Railroad companies got tired o' being took . . .' the old man paused as a hideous, wracking cough shook his spare frame.

'So they offered a big reward for ol' Levi and any of the boys,' he went on weakly. 'Big enough to set me hunting them. I caught Thad, the younker, in Brownsville, and had to kill 'im and then I followed 'em around the state, for 'bout a year. And they allus seemed to fetch up in Waco's Find, but I could never get a line on where their hideout might be. Not 'til one night, when . . . this fella paid me a visit.' Hewitt paused, trying to gather strength, but his voice was very low as he went on and Wheeler had to place an ear next to the old man's lips to catch his next words.

'Tol' me the gang was on to me. Comin' fur me that night. Offered to lay fer 'em . . . split . . . reward. So we did, me and him, Ed Harris . . . coupla others.' Hewitt managed to gasp out.

'This fella . . . knew where . . . gonna . . . leave . . . horses. . . . Killed 'em all bar Levi and three o' the boys and they was shot tryin' to escape after . . . trial.'

'And what kept you hangin' around?' Wheeler asked. He felt Hewitt's painful shrug in the darkness.

'Levinson's . . . cache. Figgered . . . must . . . be . . . lot. Me and my partner . . . lookin' on and off . . .' the old man managed.

'And he tried to kill me them times?' Wheeler asked. 'Or was dosing that stallion your idea?'

'Nope, his'n,' the old man groaned in the darkness. 'How'd you . . . know . . . not . . . Blagg . . . like . . . I . . . to' . . . you?'

Wheeler shrugged. 'Horse-dopin' is common wherever you go but a city fella like Blagg or any of his boys knowing about a mixture the Apache use?' he explained. 'Naw, that had to be a Westerner and an old-timer at that. Sure, nearly got me though.' There was no reply and Wheeler wondered how long he had been talking to himself. Gently, he disengaged the old man's hand.

'*Vaya con Dios*, Horse-thief,' he said gently, 'Now I better see about getting out of here. Wonder where that breeze is comin' from?'

Searching the floor of the cave for one of the discarded pine-knots and some twigs took time but Wheeler dared not use any of his scanty store of matches. Eventually, his persistence paid off and he managed to gather together a small supply of discarded kindling. Three of his precious matches were spent before his tiny fire was burning satisfactorily.

'I hope I ain't wastin' my time,' Wheeler muttered as he carefully touched the resiny pine-knot to the nearest flame. It flared immediately and as Wheeler shifted it cautiously above his head, the little flame flickered and jumped in a sudden, all but undetectable breath of air. Wheeler gave a grunt of satisfaction and began a minute inspection of the solid-looking back wall of the cave. Not many minutes had passed before his patience was rewarded.

The breeze was coming from a substantial-looking crack at the back of the cave. It was barely big enough to let him squeeze through but beyond the narrow opening, Wheeler could plainly see a second, larger cave and, more encouraging still, a distant glimmer of light.

Swiftly, wedging his pine-knot in a convenient crack, Wheeler made a rapid search of his late victims' bodies, which revealed more matches, and a double handful of cartridges which would not fit either of his weapons. With a shrug, he pocketed them and moved swiftly back to the crack.

After a muscle-cracking stretch, he managed to wedge the torch securely in another fissure a little way above his head, on the other side of the opening. This done, he eased his body into the crack and, grunting with effort, made to force his way through. But it was no use. The rock refused to yield and Wheeler found himself inches too thick.

Savagely, he dragged himself back and tried again, only to be repulsed a second time. And time was running out. His little fire was burning low and without light, he would never find the solution to the problem of escape.

For long moments, Wheeler glared at the rock, almost as if it were an opponent he could daunt with a glare. Then he snapped his fingers.

'Mebbe,' he wondered aloud, 'just mebbe. . . .'

Swiftly, he tore off his clothes, all but the boots. Guns, Levis, hat, coat even the bandanna were pushed through the gap, then Wheeler wedged himself into position and began to heave. Three times he strained against the unyielding rock and then suddenly something cracked, his feet slipped and he was through, minus much of the skin from his ribs and chest. But through!

As he roughly pulled on his clothes, Wheeler made a swift survey of this new prison. What he saw didn't inspire much hope. There was certainly a hole, fairly high up on the rock face, although it looked an easy climb, on the litter of boulders and rubbish strewn across the floor. But it was plain that climbing up would have been pointless. The hole through which the afternoon sun percolated wasn't big enough to admit his head, let alone his whole body!

Wheeler, however, refused to be disheartened. Working swiftly he built a low, wide cairn of stones which enabled him to reach up and explore the exterior of the hole. As his groping fingers whisked over the outside of the rock, new hope began to dawn. The material that made up the hole was barely the thickness of Wheeler's clutching fingers and as he dragged at the opening handfuls of the soft pumice simply flaked away. Hardly daring to believe his luck, Wheeler raked and pulled until, at the end of an hour's hard digging, he found himself up against a ridge of hard rock that wouldn't budge. He slumped back, dejected, but a fresh examination, carried out from the floor of the cave, showed him that all that barred the hole from being useful was a boulder, perhaps a foot round, which, projecting into the side of the hole, prevented his exit.

A rapid survey confirmed his suspicions and, more worryingly, showed that the stone was fixed apparently immovably. There were certainly a number of cracks between this stone and the rock face proper, one even being fairly deep, but not deep enough to compromise the join between them.

'I need a good pick or some goddam blasting powder,' Wheeler snarled to himself. Then he stopped and began to feel through his pockets. He didn't have giant powder but. . . .

Suddenly his hand closed on the collection of cartridges he had taken from Wint's belt.

In the sparse, slanting sunlight now filtering through his widened hole, Wheeler spread his old bandanna and went to work. Using his knife, he carefully prised the slug out of each of the cartridges and poured their contents into the centre of the cloth. With all the rounds emptied, he found himself with enough gunpowder to half fill his fist. Doubtfully, he inspected it, before pulling the rest of his own cartridges from their belt loops and adding that powder to the pile.

Satisfied at last, Wheeler knotted the ends of the bandanna into a neat and powder-tight parcel which, after much effort, he managed to wedge tight at the bottom of the deepest crack. It was the work of only moments to wedge stones around the parcel until a bare square inch of gaudy bandanna remained in view, then he stepped back and taking a deep breath, drew his Sibley Colt.

A dozen times, Wheeler raised the long-barrelled pistol, squinting carefully along the sights and each time he was forced to lower the weapon unsteadily and stand back, his grip tightened and vision misted. Finally, dashing sweat from his eyes, he lost his temper, jerked his arm up and let fly.

The big revolver cracked once but to no effect, and Wheeler heard the bullet whine off stone on its way God knew where. A second time he fired, still with no result, but the third shot was greeted almost instantly by a roaring crack and a huge cloud of dust, then . . . nothing.

He stood aghast. It hadn't worked. Goddam it, it hadn't worked. Covered in dust and filth, Wheeler could have wept. But, almost instantly, his resolve hardened.

Carefully, he shoved away the Colt and its two precious cartridges, climbed on to the rock pile he had made and grasped at the offending stone, intending to lever himself up. But the rock held for only a brief moment, before slipping out of the hole.

Unable to save himself, Wheeler slipped backwards, off the rock pile, while the boulder, with malign intelligence, smashed down on to his side, bruising the muscles and neatly cracking two of his short ribs.

Instantly, the pain took hold and he blacked out, but it lasted only moments and he came to to find himself looking up into a hole big enough to admit two good-sized men. He shifted, wincing at the shaft of pain, then spat accurately into the palm of his hand. It was clear, no blood, and with a grunt of effort, Wheeler eased round and began to make a cursory inspection of his injuries by feel.

CHAPTER FIFTEEN

The damage proved less than Wheeler might have expected. A couple of strips torn from his ragged shirt and bound in place allowed him to breathe with only slight discomfort.

Gingerly, he eased himself upright, grimacing as the ribs twinged, but once on his feet, things didn't seem quite so bad.

'Probably only hurt when I laugh,' Wheeler told himself, 'and I ain't likely to be doin' too much o' that for a while.'

As swiftly as his injuries allowed, Wheeler rebuilt the cairn he had used for his excavation, stacking the rocks and crumbling rubbish as high up the wall as he could reach.

At last, unable to make the pile any higher, he stood back and began carefully to check the action and the loads of both the long-barrelled Sibley and the double-action Smith & Wesson. Things certainly could have been better. He had two left in the Colt, one in his second pistol. And that was all.

'Guess I won't go bear hunting jus' yet awhile,' he

thought, before rapidly sobering. 'Just hope the bears feel the same way.'

What little light had been filtering into the hole was fading fast as Wheeler climbed awkwardly on to his rock pile for the last time. Clumsily, he felt for hand-holds but the crumbling sandstone, which had been so convenient to dig, now allowed him no purchase for the climb out. Finally, brute strength and a minuscule fingerhold in the rock dragged his feet off the rock pile. By dint of much kicking and scrambling he managed to lever himself through the hole. And right into more bad news.

His oh so convenient hole turned out to be not so convenient at all. It opened into the bottom of a narrow ravine whose sheer sides reared up four or five times the height of a man. Now it was clear why the sunlight shining through the hole had been so fitful. Even calling the place a ravine was complimentary, since Wheeler barely needed to stretch if he wished to reach across the space between the opposite walls. Two men couldn't have squeezed in side by side. And just to add what seemed a final insult, as he inspected the rough yellow walls the sun slipped past the lip of the crack and plunged the whole place into a fitful twilight.

'Jesus Christ and all his goddam b. . . . .d angels!' Wheeler swore with feeling. There really didn't seem to be much more to say.

His choices, however, were clearly laid out in front of him. Either he climbed the rock and tried to locate Hassan and the cache of food and cartridges or he lay down at the bottom of that damned hole until he died.

'And I still got a coupla few things to do before I

hand in my checks,' he told himself, with killing Horse-thief Hewitt's ex-partner right slap bang at the top of the list.

Of all the difficulties and dangers he had encountered on this job so far, climbing out of that sandstone crack was probably the worst. He had no way of securing himself against a fall and his ribs burnt like fire as, with his back firmly wedged against the rock wall, he drove first one leg against the opposite face and then the other, fighting the rock as though it were an enemy.

He had managed almost half the distance, fifteen feet from the floor and quite high enough to ensure a broken back, when his foot slipped.

With one leg freed of all restraint and flailing in space, he tried desperately to stiffen the anchored leg. Just as it seemed that his abused joints could stand no more, his hand found a narrow, jutting spur. Instantly, he threw his weight upon it, only to feel it crumble to nothing under his desperately clutching fingers, just as the heel of his other boot jammed itself into a lucky and convenient crevice.

For a while, he dared not even breathe, sure that the slightest movement would plunge him to a painful and lingering death on the rock floor below. Breath and common sense began to come back at about the same time, however, and soon he had recovered enough to try the next part of the climb.

Thankfully, this proved much easier, as the ravine narrowed considerably towards the top and he was able to more or less scramble up the last few feet.

As he lay on the clean, hard rock, drawing air deep into his tortured lungs, the sun dipped red behind the peaks, throwing a shaft of orange light towards him, as if in farewell. And just to remind him that his little mountain trip still had one or two surprises left in store, a low, throbbing scream floated across the still, hot air. Like a woman in endless torment it sounded, but Wheeler had caught the beginning, heard the 'Cou. . .gar' that gave the animal its common South-Western name. Bleakly, he surveyed the surrounding peaks as the light left them and he loosened the Colt in its long holster. If ol' Soft-foot wanted to play games, he might find he'd bitten off more than he could chew, Wheeler told himself. Then he grinned tightly. Perhaps he could have worded that better.

His luck, for the moment, though, seemed to be in because he quickly found a plain trail leading away and down from the little plateau where the crack had led him. It looked clear of stones and the light-coloured rock made it easy to find his way, even in the swiftly descending twilight. Wheeler was under no illusion about his position. If he didn't find water and horses by the next day – the day after at the very latest – that would be the end. He couldn't remember his last drink and now his throat and chest were both burning like fire.

Time passed and the pain in his feet was growing to match the twinges in his chest, when he rounded a turn at the end of the trail, which had been narrowing for some time, only to find himself suddenly staring up at a blank rock wall. There seemed no way round or over it but as a chance reflection from the fitful moonlight swept over the surface, he could just make out a narrow ledge stretching out past the overhang. Everything else lay masked in deep, impenetrable shadow.

The ledge would have been a daunting prospect for a fit man in clear daylight but to Wheeler in his present condition it seemed impossible. And as if to remind him that he had no choice, another scream, closer than the first, split the night. The mountain lion had found his trail.

Without any further ado, Wheeler slipped off his boots, shoved them inside his tattered shirt and felt his way on to the ledge. Once there, it wasn't too hard. Or it wouldn't have been if his side would stop aching and he could have rested his arms and . . . the cougar hadn't suddenly appeared on the trail in front of him, poised delicately on the balls of her feet.

It was the scree scattered over the ledge that saved Wheeler. Even as the big cat crouched to spring, a stone shifted under its foot and it lost its balance, delaying its leap for a vital split second as Wheeler shifted his weight and, ignoring the pain in his injured side, sent his right hand driving desperately for a pistol. Before the lion could recover its balance or its wits, the Smith & Wesson roared and a flat-nosed bullet smashed into its brain. Devoid of the energy that had allowed it to remain erect, the body lost its footing and crashed down off the trail, hurtling to the rocks, only twenty feet below the feet of the man from El Paso.

Wheeler couldn't believe his eyes, until he realized that it was the even colour of the rocks and the darkness which had fooled him. Only yards away, a stand of pines reared graceful tops to the sudden moonlight and there was plainly solid, sloping earth at their bases. Gratefully, Wheeler slipped on his boots and prepared to quit mountaineering for good.

Up on the rimrock, a pair of yellow eyes watched the detective making his careful descent. Tail flicking nervously, the tom cougar shifted back the way he had come, following what remained of the blood smell.

Wheeler had little time to spare for congratulating himself on his safe descent from the mountain. He needed to locate those horses, and after a little thought it became clear that his rock chimney must at least have brought him out on the right side of the mountain. Pine-trees were uncommon this high up and he quickly realized that these must be the outlying stragglers of the trees which grew around the spring he and Hewitt had located. Had it been only two days before?

His ribs had now settled down to a dull ache that hurt only if he twisted or moved fast. Unfortunately, it also made rapid movement of his right hand nearly impossible. With a shrug, he twisted his belt until the Sibley lay convenient to his left. Comforted by the lack of pain this action produced and the two cartridges remaining in his Colt, he took a calculating glance at the lie of the land, then struck off downhill, confident that he must eventually strike the little stream which he would only have to follow to the relative safety of food and horses.

Wheeler located the water course at last a couple of hours before dawn and, satisfied that he was within easy reach of safety, he settled himself down in a convenient crevice to snatch a brief rest.

Cold and hunger roused him before the sun found the treetops but dawn was well over the nearby horns of the mountains as he came through the last of the trees overlooking the camp-ground, only to drop instantly behind a convenient tree-trunk. Rolo was limping across the clearing towards Hassan, who happened to be the nearest of the ponies. And in the woods behind the detective, yellow eyes were scanning the under-growth and a tufted tail whisked nervously as the wind bore the scent of horse to sensitive nostrils.

Wheeler flicked a glance at the rapidly lightening sky, then shifted rapidly down the slope towards the camp-ground. First to reach the horses was liable to be the winner in this game where the stakes had suddenly increased dramatically.

A night in the forest hadn't helped Rolo's nerves at all. The fat deputy was no woodsman and he had lain fear-fully awake in the discomfort of a tree while he peopled the darkness below with all the terrors that hunger and a feverish imagination could concoct. For once in his life, the predawn chill had found him awake and astir, following the course of the little stream he had encoun-tered in the hope that it might offer some inspiration. He could hardly believe his ears or his luck when he heard the complaining nicker of a horse floating across the morning air. Five minutes later, he stumbled into the little clearing and saw not one but two horses and his means of returning to town.

Cautiously, he worked downwind of the stocky grey. He could see no saddle but beggars, after all, could not be choosers and there was a picket line which would do for an improvized bridle. Hardly daring to breathe he worked almost to within hand's reach of the rope, when Hassan jerked backwards, snatching the rope away.

Time and again the fat man crept within inches, only to have the little horse turn and trot a few yards out of reach, looking back as if daring the man to try again. Patience and temper had long since departed when, throwing all caution aside, Rolo lurched to his feet and lumbered desperately after the stocky Arab. But this was a game Hassan liked to play and it wasn't long before Rolo pitched exhausted into the grass and lay listening to the sound of his own heart trying to beat its way out through his ears.

'If'n you'all have finished your little game, mebbe we could get back to town. I got business with your boss and the marshal,' said a sardonic voice not very far away. Rolo looked up. Wheeler was standing some feet from Rolo, with Hassan's picket line coiled negligently in his hand, while the little grey snatched mouthfuls of grass from around his boots.

Horror held Rolo immobile and he could only splutter:

'B . . . b . . but how? I seen the rock come down myself. You was buried, you're dead! You gotta be!' he finished unreasonably.

Wheeler shrugged. 'Like Mr Twain's,' he sneered, 'reports of my death have been greatly exaggerated, etcetera.' Seeing the look of incomprehension on the fat face in front of him, he said: 'Never mind. We got business somewhere else.' Wheeler gestured and Rolo became aware of the big Colt in the detective's left hand. Left hand? And that gunbelt didn't hang like it oughta.

In Rolo's cunning brain, a little bell began to ring.

There might still be a way out.

CHAPTER SIXTEEN

'Get on your feet, fatso,' Wheeler ordered, gesturing with his pistol as he walked forward. 'If you want to try anything, go ahead. I'd as soon take you in across a saddle. You'll be less trouble that way.'

Slowly, Rolo staggered to his feet, left hand concealed behind his back. An evil grin lit his face as he shook his head.

'No, you wouldn't,' he stated confidently. 'You got to have me alive to prove you didn't shoot the girl. You need me alive,' he repeated, 'but I don't need you!'

As the words were spat from his lips, Rolo was in motion, leaping at his intended victim and swinging up the stone he had held concealed in his hand. Slowed by hunger and fatigue, Wheeler jerked up his right hand, causing his ribs to rack him with pain, slowing his response. Rolo's rock slammed past his weakened guard and smashed sickeningly into his head. Luckily, his battered sombrero caught most of it but the blow knocked him to the ground, still conscious, although unable to make so much as a move in his own defence.

But Rolo was more concerned with escape and his own skin. A lucky snatch secured the rope around the neck of a surprised Hassan and in an instant, Rolo had scrambled aboard.

'I sure wish I had time to spare for . . .' Rolo began. Whatever he had been about to say was lost in a yelp of surprise as a furious Hassan snapped round and ripped a six-inch strip of leather from one of Rolo's dilapidated boots. But the man had no time to bemoan his loss. Barely pausing for breath, the fighting-mad stallion whirled across the open space, sunfishing, bucking and, in between, trying to chew his rider to pieces, until with a vicious flick, he unseated Rolo and threw him hard against the thick trunk of a tall pine tree on the edge of the clearing. Not content with that, the little horse snatched round and thundered towards the two-legged thing that had had the temerity to try and ride him, clearly intent upon stamping it to unrecognizable fragments.

Hassan was barely two long paces from his intended victim when a clear, piercing whistle split the air and the little grey slid to a halt. He shook his head and turned to trot back to his master, who was already limping across the clearing to meet him.

'Like I said, you fat bastard, get on your fe . . .' Wheeler began. Then he stopped, because behind the prone, breathless figure of Rolo, the big tom cougar stepped out of the undergrowth and into the sunlight.

For a moment, the big cat stood confused, then, smelling the blood seeping from Rolo's cuts and bruises, it screamed once and sprang towards the deputy.

Wheeler was all of fifteen yards from the pair as the big cat began to move. Desperately, he threw up his left arm and touched off a shot, simultaneously breaking into an awkward, limping run. Luck or the good god that watches over pirates, hoodlums and reprobates in general must have guided his aim because the bullet smashed into the trunk of the pine tree, bare inches from the cougar's snarling face. The animal jerked back, giving the terrified Rolo time to thrust up and away. The vicious taloned paw which was meant to tear the fat man's head from his shoulders ripped across his chest from shoulder to stomach instead. Confused by the sunlight and driven half-mad with hunger and the blood smell, the angry tom reared back snarling, just as Wheeler skidded to a halt, aimed hastily and fired.

Too hastily as it turned out because the bullet missed completely, only clipping a twig inches above the animal's head. But, this time, the cougar had had enough. Frightened by the noise and the light and finding spirited resistance where he had expected an easy kill, he turned and fled, leaving Wheeler to holster his long-barrelled Colt with a sigh of relief. And find himself faced by a whole new set of problems, the first of which seemed to be bleeding to death only yards away from him.

'That lard-arsed sonofabitch was sure right about one thing,' Wheeler muttered as he limped towards the unconscious Rolo. 'Ain't nobody gonna believe a word less'n I bring him in alive.'

Rolo returned to full consciousness just as Wheeler was fastening the last of the clumsy bandages which were all he had been able to contrive from the limited range of materials available. The fat man's face was the colour of dirty milk and, typical of his coward's heart, he woke up screaming.

'Where is it? God, where is it?' he demanded, after the first fit had passed and he found himself in no immediate danger.

Wheeler shrugged. 'Back up there aways, I'd guess,' he offered. 'Don't worry,' he continued, seeing the fear and shock in the other's eyes. 'My last shot scared him off and he ain't gonna be doin' a lot of movin' in daylight.' The fear began to slide out of Rolo's eyes, to be replaced by curiosity.

'Why didn't you leave 'im get me?' the fat man demanded, plainly forgetting his previous words.

'Don't know,' Wheeler admitted honestly. 'Just couldn't, I guess.'

'I wouldn't ha' done the same for you, you know that, don't you?' Rolo stated frankly.

'Sure, I know.' Wheeler nodded. 'Now can you answer one o' my questions?' he asked mildly.

Rolo grinned tightly. 'Guess I owe you that much,' he said.

'OK.' Wheeler began, grinning back despite himself. 'Why's Blagg mixed up in this?'

'He needs money, a lot of money,' Rolo answered simply. 'He was in 'Paso last year on a trip and he heard somethin' that meant land in this part o' the country was gonna be worth a fortune. Somehow he found out what land, don't ask me how, and he's been buyin' up the whole section like it was going out of style. Hell, he's got mortgages on just about every business in town as well. I ain't sure,' Rolo grimaced as pain knifed him, 'but I think unless the deal goes through soon, the

141

bank'll call his note and he'll go under. Guess he thought his luck was in when Collins blabbed about Levinson's cache to one of his girls.' Rolo paused, grimacing as the pain took hold.

'So did you ever get Collins to talk?' Wheeler asked.

'Naw.' Rolo shook his head weakly. 'Day or two after Blagg found out about the cache, Collins vanished. The fat man fell back on to his blanket. 'Jesus,' he moaned, 'I ain't feelin' so good.'

Wheeler stood up and instinctively loosened the now reloaded Colt in its holster.

'Guess we gotta try and get back to town,' he offered mildly. 'Otherwise, looks like Blagg and Fowler takes the hand.'

Three days later, a pearly, predawn light was softening the harsh outlines of the main street of Waco's Find, as two leg-weary ponies plodded slowly up the dusty trail that led past the first of the town's rickety dwellings. Spitefully, one of the riders pulled his mount to a halt and his companion, taken by surprise, moved a few paces on before pulling up his own mount and turning in the saddle.

'What d'you stop for?' Blagg demanded.

' 'Cause I figure it might be better if we get our story straight before anyone sees us,' Fowler sneered. 'Unless, o' course, you want to be answering a lot o' damn fool questions,' he finished.

Blagg shook his head vehemently.

'When d'you figure to open that?' he asked diffidently. Fowler ignored him and the fat saloonkeeper relapsed into a frightened silence.

The journey back to town had been something of an

eye-opener for Rich Blagg. He'd had little to do with the marshal before this trip and had always regarded Fowler as a fool and office-filler. Now, he knew better. His new partner had displayed a ruthlessness which had terrified Blagg to the depths of his weak, shallow little soul and as he followed Fowler towards a run-down adobe where they could hide the horses, he began to realize that his share of Levinsons's cache might be his life and nothing more. If he was lucky.

Fowler didn't offer to speak until he and Blagg were sitting in the latter's well-furnished office behind the saloon.

Once there, the marshal leaned back in the room's only comfortable chair and said, with an expansive smile:

'Well, Rich, ol' fella, we got the dollars and I guess that leaves us holding all the aces.'

'Why, it sure does, Marv,' Blagg agreed nervously. 'What you plannin' to do with your share?'

'Share?' Fowler asked softly. 'What . . . share?'

Moments passed, pregnant with menace, until with a heavy sigh, Fowler went on:

'Rich, Rich, I can see that you're in need of a li'l education on this subject.' He paused, apparently considering the drawn, doughy features of the terrified man before him.

'I want you to listen to me now, Rich, you fat yeller bastard,' Fowler continued easily, 'so's we understand each other and there ain't no confusion. This money's mine. I deserve it on account of it was me who set Levinson up that night he was caught. Ol' bastard thought he was smart,' Fowler went on, voice rising, apparently oblivious of his terrified audience. 'But I sure fixed him. Fixed him good. Shot him in the . . . myself the night I let . . . he got out of that jail. Thought he was smart,' Fowler's voice dropped sinisterly and the light of madness waxed in his eyes, 'sending the location of the cache to that li'l bastard Collins! Tryin' to cheat me! Me, who should have had it all! But I fixed 'em . . . fixed 'em both. . . .' He finished smugly, appearing to notice Blagg for the first time.

'That little son of a bitch Collins worked for Levinson, used to feed him information about banks and railroads,' he explained. 'Come down here lookin' for the cache and figurin' to try a little blackmail on his own account, I guess. Thought he was smart. Wouldn't tell where Levinson hid his loot when I asked him. I ain't gonna tell you what happened to him,' Fowler assured his listener, ' 'cause I want you to sleep good nights. But you want to remember this, if'n you don't remember anything else,' Fowler growled, leaning forward so that the light of malice in his eyes seemed to Blagg a living thing. 'I ain't a good man to cross.' He leaned back in the chair again, steepling his fingers and the usual bland, expansive smile was back on his face as he said:

'Now, just you trot out them deeds and stuff you bin collectin' so hard. And don't bother to deny it, Rich. I heard about that railroad spur too, see, and you ain't bin exactly clever or careful about coverin' your tracks. And don't forget the mortgage paper you're holding on Ed Harris's store and the other places around town.' The smile was still there but Fowler's eyes glittered as he said: 'After all, Rich, partners ought to be able to trust each other.'

Obediently, Blagg turned to his safe, desperately cramming down his elation. Fowler had said that Collins came down here to blackmail someone. That had been a mistake on the marshal's part. Blagg had been involved in enough of that sort of dirty business to realize that the only person who could have known Collins had blackmail in mind was the potential victim.

And it went without saying, the fat saloonkeeper thought to himself, that if Collins had been smart enough to find Fowler's little secret, it shouldn't take Rich Blagg any time at all.

CHAPTER SEVENTEEN

That evening, the barroom of the Busted Dollar looked set for another brisk night's business. Yellow lamplight bounced from the rows of bottles with their ornate labels, to be caught and thrown back by the cheap jewellery and brassy decoration on the dresses of the saloon-girls entertaining the early dribble of customers, which looked set to soon turn into its usual nightly flood.

Standing on the crude balcony that overlooked the barroom, Rich Blagg might have been forgiven for feeling a touch of pride in the monster he had created. But the saloon and its inhabitants were the last thing occupying his mind tonight.

Anxiously, he scanned the crowd, looking for a particular face, then he cursed, foul and low-voiced as the batwings flipped back and a figure, wearing the star of a town marshal and carrying a battered carpet-bag still strapped with its original rope, sauntered through them and across to the bar. With a snarl that was three parts fear, Blagg blundered along the balcony, fetching up at the bar just as Fowler was lifting a glass to his thick fleshy lips.

Without any attempt at restraint, Blagg grabbed his elbow, slopping the glass's contents over the marshal's hand as he hissed:

'Christ, ain't you opened it *yet?*' For one long second, Fowler looked down at his hand, from which the liquor still dripped, until slowly his eyes rose, boring hard into those of the fat saloonkeeper. Suddenly, his liquor-drenched hand slashed upwards, catching Blagg across the face and knocking him to the floor, where he lay, half stunned, and smeared with the filthy sawdust.

In the sudden, intense silence that followed the blow, Fowler's voice sounded unnaturally loud.

'See, here's the thing, Rich,' Fowler began affably, although there was the mad glitter of a sunstruck rattler in his eyes as he turned back to the bar and signalled for another drink, 'in all partnerships, there's a junior partner and a senior partner.' He smiled benignly down at the discomfited saloonkeeper and the mad glitter deepened as he went on:

'Guess you're clear about which is which now?'

Ignoring the sawdust-covered Blagg as he struggled to his feet, Fowler turned, still holding his drink, and placed his back to the bar.

'Now, I want all you men to hear this! Me and Rich are going into partnership.' He nodded across at the terrified saloonkeeper, 'and on account o' that, me and my new partner want you all to have a drink with us. You!' Fowler snapped at the Dollar's head bartender, 'set up drinks for everybody!'

Anxiously, the man licked his lips, flicking a glance towards his employer. But before Blagg could move or make a sign, a mild voice drifted across the silence.

147

'I don't know about anyone else but I sure could use a drink right about now.'

Fowler jerked around in the direction of the owner of the voice and Blagg's face turned a sickly greenish-white as Cord Wheeler pushed through the crowd and came to a halt at the end of the bar, facing Fowler, the ivory-butted Smith & Wesson dangling casually from one hand.

For a moment, the scene was frozen, then some one bellowed:

'It's him, that Wheeler, the fella that murdered the whore!' Around the room, hands dropped swiftly gunwards, only to freeze as Wheeler's pistol flipped into line and fired. The bullet smashed a bottle above the head of Blagg's barkeep and Wheeler's voice was icily gentle as he moved behind the bar.

'Now, son, you just reach me up that scattergun you got down there, then you get lost. I got somethin' to say and I reckon that scatter'll keep the folks quiet while I say it.'

Being careful to hold the weapon only by its barrels, the barkeep gingerly handed it over before gratefully jumping the bar to the safety and anonymity of the crowd. Wheeler nodded, swiftly checked the loads in the wicked-looking, short-barrelled weapon before cocking it and placing it on the bar facing Marv Fowler.

'Now we're all pretty comfortable,' he began, dextrously opening a bottle of beer against the bar-top and sampling its contents without once losing the drop. 'I want to tell you all a little story.'

In a few words, he outlined the reasons behind his journey to Waco's Find.

'But Miss Mona, she never quite sat right as a surveyor's wife,' Wheeler explained, 'and when she described the fella she called Collins, why, I recognized him right off. Especially, being as he was nosin' around the town where Levinson was caught.'

Briefly, he reiterated Royston's sordid history. Before he could finish, Ed Harris broke in:

'I remember him,' the little storekeeper stated. 'Seems like I recall there was considerable talk in the El Paso papers about why someone like Royston would have anything to do with an old deadbeat like Levi.'

Wheeler nodded agreement. 'Sounds reasonable,' he offered. 'Anyhow, Royston done his best but Levinson, as most folks know, was convicted, sentenced to hang and got killed tryin' to escape. Royston went to jail shortly afterwards for . . . somethin' else and when he got out he trailed down here.'

'This is all real interestin',' Fowler snapped, 'but perhaps you could get to the point and then we'll get on with hanging you!' For a moment the eyes of the two men locked and it was the marshal's that dropped first as Wheeler said mildly:

'I wouldn't talk so free and easy about hanging if I was you, lard ass. Ever hear tell of the biter bit?' Receiving no answer, he continued:

'Now, one thing I couldn't figure was how Collins or Royston got down here so quick and appeared to be livin' so well. He'd bought surveyor's tools, a train-ticket. All takes money and, believe me, coin to spare ain't something an ex-con has much of. So someone was stakin' him. Since Royston never had a friend in the world, that only left blackmail. But who?' Wheeler

149

spread his hands and a slow smile crept across his face.

'Then I did something I should have been doin' all along. I started thinking. Firstly, outlawin' ain't a profession with what you'd call a secure future. Not many gangs last more'n five years, mostly they last a lot less. But Levi Levinson and his boys were hellin' up this country for more like fifteen. Never even a sniff o' them bein' caught. How'd they last so long? And then I remembered something else I'd heard. Seems Levinson and his boys was famous for never bustin' a dud. Any stage or train or bank they took was allus worthwhile. Don't take a genius to figure they must've had an inside man.'

Wheeler shifted along the bar towards Fowler, carelessly gesturing with his pistol as he went.

'Someone with a good excuse for being down here regular and who had access to information about gold shipments and that kinda thing. I figure Collins knew who he was and he forced the fella to stake him.'

'Hell,' Fowler blurted. 'It could have been anyone. Some railroad shipping-clerk out for easy money. Even this . . . Royston hisself.'

'Nope.' Wheeler shook his head. 'That'd fit if they just hit railroads or banks or sich, but Levinson, hell, he took all sorts. And there's only one set o' folks know more about where money's going than outlaws and that's the people who got to look after it.'

'Lawmen,' Harris breathed softly.

'That's right.' Wheeler nodded agreement. 'More than that, federal lawmen, 'cause local law never knows anything 'til it's too late. What did you do before you was appointed marshal, Fowler?' he asked suddenly.

'He was a federal deputy,' Harris supplied softly, 'and now I come to think of it, it sure was funny how often he come down here huntin' outlaws by hisself!'

'Pah,' Fowler snorted, waving his hand as if to sweep aside the nets he felt closing in. 'You were right in the first place, Wilson or whatever your name is. This is just a story and you can't prove none of it.' He glared round at the circle of suddenly threatening faces.

'I'm still the goddamn marshal o' this burg and what I say goes,' Fowler cursed, voice rising towards a scream. 'And I think it's long gone time this saddle bum was locked up!'

Reluctantly, Ed Harris stepped forward, coming to a halt beside the marshal. The little storekeeper's voice was gentle as he said:

'Much as I hate to admit it, but this fat bastard's got a point. Less'n you got somethin' else to say, that is.'

Wheeler nodded.

'Just one thing, and when I've said that, if'n you ain't convinced, waal, I'll take myself to jail,' he offered, drawing a long, unsteady breath.

For a moment, everything hung in the balance, then Harris nodded.

'Say your say,' he ordered. 'As justice o' the peace I'm authorizing it.' Harris tapped the worn black butt of the Colt Peacemaker holstered in the greasy, cut-away holster at his side. 'Judge Colt presiding,' he concluded with a mirthless grin.

Wheeler's answering smile was equally cold.

'I'm sure thanking the judge,' he began lightly, then his voice dropped and it took on a note of arctic chill. 'Some of you may be wonderin' what happened to

151

Collins. Well, I can tell you 'cause I found his body up in the mountains. He was murdered, cut up worse than an Apache squaw could ha' done it. The man that did it is there.' Wheeler snapped a finger at Fowler. 'And I can prove it.'

'Prove it, hell,' Fowler snorted with an assurance he was far from feeling. 'You've just about played out your string and you're saying anything that'll get between you and a rope!'

'Naw,' Wheeler said softly, fumbling in his pocket as he came round the bar and walked towards Fowler.

'I found this in his hand.' He stopped and held up a shred of gold braid. 'You all seen that fancy New Orleans vest the marshal's so proud of. Well, I'm bettin' this piece'll fit somewhere on that vest. Not very long, is it?' Wheeler addressed the marshal. 'But it'll be big enough to hang you!'

For one tense second, Fowler's face twisted; fear, hatred and loathing chasing in turn across his countenance. Then he laughed in relief.

'Hell, it's a trick,' he began, 'I wasn't even wearing that vest on the day . . .' Fatally, too late, he realized what he had said.

'That's right; like you said, you wasn't wearing the vest that day,' said Wheeler. 'I cut this from a piece I found in Harris's store before I come in here, but finish what you was gonna say, Marshal, it sounded real interestin'.'

Slowly, the big man's face swept round the crowd. In every face he saw death written plain and he returned last of all to the man who had outwitted and outplayed him.

'Guess you think you're pretty smart, don't you,' Fowler demanded, raising his left sleeve to pull at the cuff. 'Well, you're wrong. Dead wrong.' The last two words were a scream as Fowler's left hand jerked forward and the derringer slapped into his palm.

The smashing report of two shots filled the bar-room, so close together as to be almost one, then Fowler was falling forward, clutching at his blood-spouting belly while his intended victim curiously inspected the gore seeping slowly from a hole in his left arm.

'Guess I'll take that drink now,' Wheeler said, turning unsteadily towards the bar.

'Drink! *Drink!*' Rich Blagg seemed unable to believe his ears. 'Goddamn whiskey! Don't nobody want to see what's in that bag?'

CHAPTER EIGHTEEN

'I guess you got a right to look,' Wheeler said softly, 'but I got a feelin' you ain't gonna find what you expect.'

But Blagg wasn't listening. He was down on hands and knees scrabbling at the rope bindings on the bag. Suddenly he realized he was getting nowhere and glared wildly around.

'A knife, give me a damn knife, fer Christsake.' Harris bent swiftly, a blade flashed in his hand and the rope bindings fell away as Blagg wrenched the bag open.

For a moment he scrabbled eagerly, then he reached into the bag and drew out a piece of rolled parchment, only to fling it aside as he stared in disbelief at the bag's contents.

Slowly, fat face a green-tinged mask of incomprehension, Blagg tipped the bag on its end, allowing its contents to sift on to the floor. There was no gold, no bills, instead the floorboards were covered with a collection of rocks and the pale, sifting, alkali dust of the South-West.

'Nothing,' Blagg intoned, like a child mouthing a poorly understood lesson. 'Nothing?'

'It wouldn't have helped you even if there'd been any money there,' Wheeler informed him from his position on the bar where he had been interestedly watching the blood dripping from his arm in a sluggish stream and turning the dusty floor an attractive shade of saffron. The sawn-off lay, forgotten, on the bar between them.

'Federal authorities would've impounded it,' Harris told him. 'You should've opened it somewhere quiet.'

Despairing, Blagg glared from one to the other of the two men as Wheeler continued mildly:

'And that ain't the end o' your troubles.' He jerked his chin at the door. 'I got Rolo out there, slung behind a horse. I don't figure he's gonna live much longer, on account of a cougar rippin' half his chest skin off, and the infection an' all, but he told me enough to hang you about ten times over.' Awkwardly, he reached into a pocket and drew out a neatly folded piece of paper.

'So I wrote it all down and he's signed it. I figure he'll last 'til we get it attested by Harris and a coupla these upstandin' citizens.' Wheeler bestowed a benign smile on the saloonkeeper.

Slowly, moving like an old man, Blagg staggered to his feet. His face still glowed with its greenish tinge and absently he wiped both hands from nose to chin, massaging his heavy jowls thoroughly, as though to wash away the memory of the past. His hands still hovered over his mouth when he spoke, giving his voice a hollow ring.

'I guess you think you got me,' he said carefully, look-ing directly at Wheeler. The detective shrugged; all the answer needed or apparently looked for because Blagg nodded and turned slowly towards the bar.

Too late, Wheeler realized his intention as with a speed unusual in a fat man, Blagg swept the sawn-off from its place on the bar, spinning full circle and menacing Wheeler with the twin barrels. Tired, wounded and caught flat-footed though he was, Wheeler still managed to blow out a gusty, contemptuous breath.

'So what now?' he demanded gently.' You got two shots in that thing, no horses and even if you managed to get out of town, you'd be lost and starving in a day, if you lived that long. Put it down, Fatso. I hear tell hanging ain't so painful.'

For a long second fear and hatred chased each other across Blagg's face, then with a scream of bestial rage, he snapped up the shotgun and pulled the trigger. But Wheeler had been gambling on just such a reaction and even as the gun began to move, he pushed himself on to the elbow which rested on the bar and, using this as a pivot, swung his legs and lower body smoothly on to the polished timber, allowing the buckshot to smash harmlessly into the place where his body had been a bare split second before.

Stunned into disbelief, Blagg stared first at the weapon in his hand and then at the grinning figure on the bar-top.

'You lose again,' Wheeler offered, as Ed Harris stepped forward, Colt in hand.

'I'll take that,' Harris ordered, holding out his free hand.

Stupidly, Blagg looked at the outstretched hand, then he jerked the twin tubes up, crammed them into his mouth and pulled the trigger, a split second before Ed Harris's shot drove into his chest, smashing the body with its hideous head wound back into the bar.

Without a glance at the dead man, Harris turned to the crowd.

'Someone drag that outta here,' he snapped. Before he could add anything, a man kneeling at Fowler's side looked up and said:

'Marshal's alive, Ed.'

'Get him into one of the rooms upstairs,' the little man ordered. He turned to Wheeler, who was now gingerly climbing down from the bar. 'Guess we better see after Rolo,' he offered.

Wheeler shrugged. 'Only need a shovel,' he said callously. 'Died this mornin'. Never did really come to properly except the once, after the cat got 'im.

'And the confession?' Harris snapped.

'Oh, that. Look for yourself,' Wheeler said, tendering the piece of paper.

'El Paso Grande,' Harris read aloud, then looked up. 'This is a hotel bill,' he said. 'There ain't nothin' on here about what Blagg done.' He looked, uncomprehending, at Wheeler.

'It sure is,' Wheeler assured him. 'A very expensive hotel bill. But, believe me,' he emphasised, 'the lady was worth every penny.'

But Harris wouldn't be deflected.

'You tricked him into killin' hisself.' Harris continued accusingly. 'You knew there wasn't a thimbleful o' evidence agin him, so you tricked him into killin' hisself. Why?'

But Wheeler didn't answer. He was thinking about a

girl lying in a dark street, her body full of laudanum and shotgun pellets. Then he shrugged and his face was bleak as he said:

'The fat bastard'd lived too long. Way, way too long.'

Harris saw the hardness in his face and voice and said no more.

Sun-up three days later saw two men standing on the veranda of the only hotel in Waco's Find, while a patient grey stallion pulled listlessly at the reins holding him to the rickety hitch rail. Marv Fowler had died in blistering agony the night before as gut-shot men will, and Wheeler found nothing to hold him in town any longer.

'We'll be needin a new town marshal,' Harris offered diffidently. 'Could put in a word with the town council if'n you wanted to stay.'

Wheeler shook his head.

'I got business,' he said simply.

Harris nodded. 'What I can't figure,' he began thoughtfully,' is how you knew there was no money in that bag. And why in hell did you come down here in the first place if'n you knew it was a set-up?'

Wheeler looked over his shoulder, fingers busy with the bed-roll.

'The first one's easy. I knew there wasn't a cache from the time you told me about the stuff they had on their saddles. They was leavin' the country, like you said. If'n you was an outlaw, would you leave cash behind, just on the off-chance that you'd want to come back and get it?

'Naw,' Wheeler stated flatly, without bothering to

wait for an answer. 'You take everything when you run.'
He paused. 'I sure am wonderin' where Levinson may
ha' spent all that money he stole, though. Who sold
him grub and cartridges and horses an' sich?'
Inconsequentially, he went on, 'Sure a nice house you
got behind that big store o' yours. You an' some o' your
friends look right prosperous for a little piss-in-the-hole
town like this. Must be a lot o' coin floatin' around
somewhere.' He gave a knowing grin that broadened
into a smile when he saw the look of consternation on
Harris's face.

'As for the rest, it was just what you might call coincidence . . . or dumb luck.' The smile disappeared as
his face hardened.

'Royston run off with my wife while I was in prison,'
he growled. 'Left her to die in a New Orleans cathouse,
when the federal marshals got too close. If I'd have
found him, I'd have killed him.' He grinned mirth-
lessly.

'That night Mona was murdered, I'd only rode into
town to get my traps and go home, 'cause I knew he was
dead. Funny how things turn out.' Without further
comment, he jerked the reins free.

'One last thing afore you go,' Harris spoke warily.
'When did you know it was Fowler?'

Wheeler shrugged. 'From the first time I met him.
See, he slipped up,' the detective explained.' He
warned me in a roundabout way not to look for Collins,
then he said: "don't waste your time on that shyster".
Ever heard tell of a shyster surveyor?' Wheeler asked.

'No,' Harris admitted.

Wheeler nodded agreement.

'No. A "shyster" is allus a lawyer. So I figured Fowler must know who Collins really was and the only one who could know that was. . . ?'

'The man he'd come to blackmail!' Harris finished for him.

'Yep.' Wheeler nodded. 'Knowin' that, the rest was simple. Fowler had to be Horse-thief's mysterious partner and the last member of the Levinson gang. Nearly fooled me with that hideout gun, though,' he admitted as he swung on to Hassan's back.

'Wilson,' Harris called, and as the detective looked down, the storekeeper gunman said coldly, 'Don't come back. Not ever. I mean it.'

Briefly, Wheeler appeared to inspect the little man, then he grinned like a mischievous little boy.

'Mebbe,' he offered and clucked Hassan away up the street.

As Harris watched the departing figures, he suddenly became aware of a familiar melody floating on the breeze.

Someone, somewhere was whistling *Shenandoah*.